"Any idea who's behind all this?"

Meagan shook her head but didn't meet his eyes.

"Someone took a big chance coming in here when you were just riding to The Market and back."

"Maybe he thought I was going out for the evening."

"Or maybe his intent was to be waiting inside the house when you got home."

Her tight jaw and the determination in her eyes told him that was something she had already considered. And was trying hard not to think about.

Hunter stepped closer and rested a hand on her shoulder. "Tell me what you're hiding from, Meagan."

Fear filled her eyes—the same as when she had faced the reporters. And when she thought he might have overheard her conversation with Anna. But she didn't respond.

"Tell me what's going on." He kept his tone soothing, nonthreatening. "Let me help you."

Her gaze dipped to her feet, and several more moments passed. Finally, she shook her head. Whatever secrets lay in her past, she was nowhere near ready to let him in.

Carol J. Post writes fun and fast-paced inspirational romantic suspense and lives in sunshiny central Florida. She sings and plays the piano for her church and also enjoys sailing, hiking, camping–almost anything outdoors. Her daughters and grandkids live too far away for her liking, so she now pours all that nurturing into taking care of two fat and sassy cats and one highly spoiled dachshund.

Books by Carol J. Post

Love Inspired Suspense

Midnight Shadows
Motive for Murder
Out for Justice
Shattered Haven
Hidden Identity

HIDDEN IDENTITY

CAROL J. POST

H HARLEQUIN® LOVE INSPIRED® SUSPENSE

PLEASE RECYCLE
THIS PRODUCT IS RECYCLABLE

Recycling programs
for this product may
not exist in your area.

LOVE INSPIRED BOOKS

ISBN-13: 978-0-373-44682-7

Hidden Identity

Copyright © 2015 by Carol J. Post

www.Harlequin.com

Printed in U.S.A.

Humble yourselves therefore under the mighty hand of God, that He may exalt you in due time: Casting all your care upon Him; for He careth for you.

–1 Peter 5:6-7

Many thanks to Cedar Key Police Chief Virgil Sandlin
and Cedar Key Fire Chief Robert Robinson, who patiently
answered all my questions. If there's anything I didn't
get right, it certainly isn't their fault!

Thank you to my family—Mom Roberts and
Jesse, Mom Post, Kim and Jerry, Robbie and Sheri and Keith—
for your unending love and encouragement.

Thank you to my friend John, who has always believed
I could do anything I set my mind to. Someday I'll grant
your wish and make you the villain in one of my books.

Thank you to my critique partners, Karen, Dixie and Sabrina.
You've talked me off the ledge more than once.

Thank you to my editor, Rachel Burkot,
and my agent, Nalini Akolekar. You're both beyond awesome!

And thank you to Chris.
You're not only my husband, you're my best friend.

ONE

The building roar of a plane engine overwhelmed the gentler sounds of the seaside, invading the tranquility of Seahorse Key. Meagan Berry looked up from the canvas in her lap. Tension spiked through her. It wasn't just the volume. Something was wrong. As she listened, the pitch dropped, and a series of sputters interrupted the flow of sound. She laid aside the canvas and pencil to hurry down the path leading to the beach. A small plane flew several yards above the water, too low to be on course for the Cedar Key Airport.

The roar became a whine, and the nose dipped. Her pulse quickened and she froze, holding her breath. The pilot leveled it out, but a second later the plane slammed against the water, sending spray shooting twenty feet into the air.

Meagan let out a startled scream and sprinted back to snatch her phone from her camera bag. She dialed 911 while running to her boat, then made her way over the waves with her four-horse motor wide open. The plane appeared to be sitting lower in the water than when it had first crashed. It was sinking.

Panic spiraled through her, sucking the air from her lungs. Help would never arrive in time. There was no good way to die, but gasping for air as water filled the lungs had to be one of the worst.

She coasted to a stop in front of the plane and peered through the windshield, relaying what she saw to the dispatcher. There were two occupants, the pilot and a passenger. The pilot's head was cocked at an unnatural angle, his neck apparently broken. She grimaced, but forced herself to study him. If he was breathing, it was too shallow to be obvious.

The passenger was unconscious, but his chest rose and fell in a slow, steady rhythm. She steered the boat around to look through the side window. Water seemed to be rushing in from below. It swirled around the men's legs, already halfway covering their thighs. The Cedar Key Fire rescue boat would be on its way. But the plane was sinking fast. She had to do something.

She disconnected the call with the emergency operator and donned her life vest. As she prepared to leave the safety of the boat, her chest tightened, the lingering remnant of a lifelong fear of water. She brushed it aside. The man's life depended on her keeping a clear mind and acting quickly.

She threw herself over the side of the boat and into the warm Gulf water. When she reached the plane, she braced both feet against its side, gripped the door handle and pulled. Twice. It didn't budge.

When she attempted it a third time, desperation added to her efforts. She yanked with all her might, summoning a strength she didn't know she had. The door opened a crack, creaking in protest. Renewed energy spiked through her.

After several more tugs, she had the door open far enough for her to slip through. She reached for the seat belt, but the latch was jammed.

"Come on." She pressed and pulled and yanked, but the belt refused to release its prisoner.

Her heart stuttered. Time was running out. The water was already past his waist. She had to free him. She scanned the cockpit, but didn't see anything useful.

Maybe she had something. She mentally ticked through the items in her tackle box—sunscreen, rope, a waterproof flashlight and…a multi-tool. Hope surged through her. She could use the knife to cut the belt.

Moments later, she set to work, sawing until she had sliced halfway through the thick nylon. The water had risen to the man's chest. His head rolled to the side, and a groan made its way up his throat.

"Hang loose. I'm getting you out of here."

Meagan resumed sawing, her motions more frantic with every passing second. When the last thread finally let go, breath that she hadn't realized she'd been holding spilled out in a relieved sigh.

But it wasn't over yet. She still had to pull him from the plane. Then if she could get her spare life jacket on him, maybe she could free the pilot. She gently lifted the shoulder harness over the man's head, then grasped his arms and pulled. The left one came forward. A gold wedding band glistened in the sunlight. He was married, maybe even still had kids at home. People who needed him.

It took several more tugs to wrestle him through the opening. When she glanced back inside, the plane was almost full of water. Her chest clenched. She was out of time.

During the next minute, she kept the passenger afloat and watched the water rise over the pilot's face, covering his mouth, his nose and finally his eyes. She drew in several sharp, jagged gasps. The worst way to die…

No, he wasn't suffering. There was no struggle, no response at all. He was likely already dead, killed on impact, neck broken. He wasn't drowning.

She closed her eyes against a sudden wave of nausea. Weakness washed through her, and a ringing sounded in her ears, slowly building to a roar. She opened her eyes and turned. A boat was speeding toward her, nose in the air. Some distance behind was a second, quickly closing the gap.

The lead boat reached her first, carrying Cedar Key police officer Hunter Kingston. Dressed in a white T-shirt with a picture of a fish spanning his chest, he apparently wasn't on duty. But as he drew up next to her, she had to admit he looked as good out of uniform as in.

"I was fishing over on the other side of Atsena Otie Key when I heard the plane." He threw the motor into idle and dropped the anchor. "Was anyone else inside?"

"Yeah, the pilot. I'm pretty sure the impact killed him, broke his neck." At least that was what she would keep telling herself. "I didn't have time to feel for a pulse or anything."

The Cedar Key Fire rescue boat approached, its engines drowning out Hunter's next words. Wade Tanner stood at the helm, Joe Stearn next to him. After taking a few seconds to get details from her, they went to work. Joe got into the water with a plastic backboard while Wade circled around to the other side of the plane. Its wings floated on the surface of the waves, the body submerged. Wade would work to free the pilot, but it would be too late. Probably six or seven minutes had passed since he'd sunk beneath the water.

A lump formed in her throat, and she once again reined in her thoughts. She would keep focusing on the man she was able to save instead of the one she'd lost.

Within minutes, Wade and Joe would be speeding toward the marina, where an ambulance would be waiting, or possibly a helicopter. The man still might not survive, but she had done all she could. The rest was up to fate.

Before returning to her boat, she glanced back down at the plane's passenger. Joe had worked the backboard under him. His eyes were closed, but he was still breathing. And there wasn't any blood. Of course, there could be internal injuries. And broken bones. And likely a head injury, since he still hadn't regained consciousness.

Hunter followed her gaze. "You know who that is, don't you?"

Dread slid down her throat. *Please, not somebody famous.*

Hunter continued before she could answer. "Richard Daniels. He's one of our US senators."

The dread morphed to full-blown anxiety. Reporters. News cameras. She had to get out of there before they arrived. She began to swim toward her boat. It had drifted about thirty feet from where she had left it.

Hunter's voice stopped her. "Need some help?"

"I could use it." Hers was a small johnboat, and she wasn't sure she could get in without capsizing it.

Hunter helped her onto his boat, then pulled up beside hers and held it steady while she stepped in. Once she had settled onto the seat, she looked back at him, ready to offer her thanks. But her words caught in her throat. He was smiling over at her, a warmth in his gaze that she'd never seen before.

"You saved Daniels's life. You kept your head and acted fast. You should be proud."

Proud? She hadn't thought about it. But Hunter was proud of her. She could tell. And it created an odd flutter in her stomach. With that soft, sandy blond hair, those gorgeous blue eyes and the fact that he was just an all-around nice guy, she was surprised he was still single. But from what she'd heard, he was too busy to devote time to romance. Besides his full-time job with Cedar Key Police Department, he taught a middle school boys Sunday school class and had his hand in almost every volunteer activity on Cedar Key.

Yes, Hunter was a special man. A year ago she would have been interested. Now she knew better. She'd been there and done that. And had the scars to prove it.

Hunter tilted his head toward the island. "Let's get you to shore."

She followed his gaze to where a small group had gathered. When the plane went down, she'd been alone. Now three boats dotted the shoreline. With her focus on the fire guys, and their motor left idling, she hadn't even heard the others approach. At least none of them looked to be reporters.

Within moments, a low rumble filled the air and a helicopter approached to circle the island, Channel 20 News, WCJB-TV painted clearly on the side. Meagan flinched, the instinct to run and hide overpowering. Seahorse Key was covered in trees, but at low tide there would be any number of places for the aircraft to land.

She gave a couple sharp tugs on the pull rope, and her motor roared to life. As she raced toward the island, Hunter matched her speed. Ten or twelve sets of eyes watched them approach. One of the bystanders was Buddy, a local fisherman. The others she didn't know. Probably tourists.

The moment she stepped ashore, she was inundated with questions. She held up a hand. "The pilot didn't make it. The other guy's unconscious. That's all I know."

The terse answer had the intended effect. The curious

group fell back, and she hurried down the path leading to the lighthouse. Hunter followed. The chopper descended a short distance east of them and disappeared behind the trees. She corralled the urge to leave everything and run back to her boat, and instead willed herself to remain calm. But as she jammed the unfinished canvas into her portfolio case, anxiety chipped away at her composure and her hands shook.

Hunter lightly touched her forearm. "Are you all right?"

He had likely intended the gesture to be comforting. But she jumped as if she'd been burned. "I'm fine. I'm just ready to head home and get into some dry clothes." She pushed her dripping bangs aside and forced a smile.

He didn't return it. His mouth was set in a firm line. Of course he would see right through her excuses. He was a cop. And behind that handsome face was a discerning mind that wouldn't give up its quest for the truth.

She snatched up the chair and began to fold it. Hunter picked up the cloth cover and held it open.

"Tell me what's going on. What are you afraid of?"

Her heart began to pound, and moisture coated her palms. As she slid the chair into its case, she gave an uneasy laugh. "Spiders. Snakes. The usual things women are afraid of." *Drowning. Edmund.*

More than anything, Edmund. Her dream come true. How quickly dreams could become nightmares.

She tucked her portfolio case under one arm and slipped the other through the camera bag strap. Leaving Hunter to follow with the chair, she started back up the path at a full jog.

His footsteps pounded behind her. "That's not what I meant."

No, that wasn't what he meant. But it was the only

answer she could give. Her life depended on keeping her identity secret.

From everyone. Even handsome, kindhearted cops.

Especially handsome, kindhearted cops.

When they reached the beach, three people had joined the others, two loaded down with camera equipment and a third holding a microphone.

One of the tourists pointed. "That's her there."

Before Meagan could react, all attention turned to her. A camera clicked, and a DVR began to record. She threw her hand up a half second too late.

No! They couldn't put her picture on the news. The only reason she was alive was because the world believed Elaina Thomas was dead. Her hair was different, cut short and dyed dark. But her face was still the same.

"Excuse me, ma'am. Can you tell us what happened?"

With her head dipped, she placed her portfolio and camera bag into the boat, ignoring the reporter's words. Hunter loaded the chair, and she continued her tasks—pushing the boat off the beach and into the water, moving her things to make way for her wet feet, and finally stepping into the boat.

Not getting anywhere with her, the reporter turned his attention to Hunter. "Someone said the lady pulled Senator Daniels from the plane. Can you verify that?"

Meagan gripped the pull rope and started the motor. As she began to back away, Hunter's voice came to her over the rumble of the four-horse.

"She did. She's a hero." He glanced toward her, then continued. "But apparently she's a modest hero and doesn't want the recognition. I think we should respect that."

"What's her name?"

She shifted into forward, holding her breath. Hunter wouldn't give her away, would he?

He gave a noncommittal shrug. "She's not from around here."

She turned the throttle and let her breath out in a rush. The reporter would assume she was a tourist and wouldn't look any further. And since Buddy had returned to his fishing, no one on the beach knew her. At that moment, she could have kissed Hunter.

What he had said was true—she wasn't from around there. She'd been in Cedar Key all of two months. Ever since her cross-country bus trip following her middle-of-the-night escape from her psycho ex-fiancé.

It wasn't just the abuse. It was the threats to her family. And the fact that she had learned Edmund's secret. And Edmund *knew* it. So she'd had no choice. Edmund would have never let her go.

Unless she was dead.

So she'd faked a fever with the help of a heating pad, gathered up minimal belongings and disappeared. Edmund's rowboat would have been found the next day with her blood on the gunnel and her hair caught under one of the oar brackets, pulled out by the roots. There would have been only one conclusion: in her delirious state, she'd taken the boat out, hit her head, tumbled overboard and drowned. In spring-fed lakes, bodies could disappear indefinitely. Edmund knew her fear of water. And that she couldn't swim.

He had underestimated her determination. And the effectiveness of YouTube videos.

A day and a half later, she'd shown up in Cedar Key with all the accoutrements of her new life—two changes of clothes, a few toiletries, a single loved photo, a bag of cash and new IDs. And an old book of poetry, cherished because it had belonged to the closest thing to a friend she'd had in over a year.

She cast a glance back at Seahorse Key. The reporters had turned their attention from Hunter and appeared to be speaking with the woman who had ratted her out. Tension spread through Meagan's shoulders, and she shook it off. The woman didn't know anything that could hurt her. Hunter did, but he had read her fear and, without knowing her past, had chosen to protect her.

She released a sigh and turned back around. The mouth of the channel was ahead, the route that would take her home.

Home. The word didn't mean what it used to. But she had come to accept that. With no real connections to the community, home would never be any more than an address. And a temporary one at that.

The night she fled from California, she'd walked away from everything—her family, her possessions, a promising art career.

But she was alive. Her mother and sister were alive.

And that was all that mattered.

Clouds hung low in a steel-gray sky, and a rain-scented breeze swept down Second Street. Another August thundershower on its way. It was only five-thirty, but already the heaviness of impending dusk had settled over Cedar Key.

Hunter walked around the corner of Tony's Seafood Restaurant. He was still in uniform and had just picked up dinner to go. Ahead of him, Meagan stepped from The Market, a plastic grocery bag hanging from each arm. Since the plane crash two weeks ago, he'd seen her a handful of times. But never alone. Maybe this was his opportunity to find out how she was doing.

She'd been in such a hurry to get off Seahorse Key. It hadn't worked. The story was big news, with variations of it airing several times. And with each clip, at some point her picture was front and center. One reporter had dubbed her "Angel in a Johnboat." The senator had even expressed a desire to find her and thank her publicly.

The problem was, Meagan Berry didn't want to be found.

Hunter passed the Tundra he'd left parked at the curb and continued down the sidewalk. But before he could reach her, a silver Intrepid pulled into the space in front of her. Anna Johnson climbed out and approached her.

"Someone came into Nature's Landing looking for you this morning."

Hunter slowed his pace, then stopped. He was close enough to hear the conversation, but Meagan hadn't yet noticed him.

"Oh, yeah?" Her tone was nonchalant. Her posture was anything but. She stood in profile, back stiff, and her face had lost three shades of color.

"Yeah. Said he was a reporter. He had a picture of you printed from that news story they did on the senator."

If Hunter wasn't sure before, now he had no doubt. With Anna's comment, the last of the blood drained from Meagan's face. She dropped both bags into the basket on the front of her bike, swung her leg over the bar and sank onto the seat.

"What did you tell him?"

"Absolutely nothing." Anna pushed her salt-and-pepper hair away from her face and continued. "I didn't like the guy. Something about him put me off the minute he walked in the door. He seemed like a tough guy, used to pushing people around and getting his own way. He threw your picture down on the counter, demanding to know whether you had stayed in any of the vacation rentals we manage. I told him I couldn't give him that information, that it was confidential."

"Thank you." Meagan's tone was heavy with gratitude. "You probably gathered from the news coverage that I'm not too crazy about reporters."

"I did. And I didn't like this one. He said that since he was a member of the press, I had to give him the information. I guess he thought if he got a little threatening, I'd be intimidated enough to spill the beans." She planted her hands on her hips and took a stubborn stance. "He underestimated this old Southerner. I don't like bullies. You bully me, and I'll just dig in my heels harder."

Hunter smiled. He hadn't seen this side of Anna before. Raised in Alabama, she was the epitome of the Southern belle. But she apparently had a stubborn streak.

She dropped her hands, then crossed her arms. "Just before he stormed out the door, I told him not to bother checking with any of the other establishments on the island, because they wouldn't tell him anything, either."

"Thank you." The gratitude was still there. "Did he happen to say what news agency he was with, or did he have a press badge?"

Creases appeared between Anna's eyebrows as she pondered the question. "No, I can't say that he did, which is odd. You would think if he was trying to throw around his status as a reporter, he would have at least flashed a badge."

"What did he look like? You know, so I can be sure to avoid him."

"Maybe five-ten, muscular, dark hair really close cropped, like a buzz cut. And he had a faint scar. Right here." She traced a short diagonal line across her cheek with one painted nail.

Meagan's eyes widened only briefly before the facade of nonchalance fell back into place. But Hunter had seen what he needed to during that brief, unguarded moment—recognition. And dread.

She gave a jerky nod. "I'll be on the lookout."

Thunder rumbled in the distance, and Anna headed into The Market. He resumed his walk down the sidewalk. Meagan wouldn't be happy if she thought he'd been eavesdropping.

He called out a greeting. "How's it going?"

Concern flashed across her features. Then she gave him a forced smile. She was probably wondering how much he had heard.

"It's good. I just rode down for some milk and eggs. I didn't have anything for breakfast tomorrow."

He cast a glance upward. The sky was darker now, the rain closer. "I can put your bike in the back of the truck and drive you home."

"Thanks, but I'm all right." She eased her bicycle into the road. A sudden flash lit up the sky, followed by a much-too-close crash, and she ducked. "Maybe I'll take you up on that."

Once seated in the truck, she folded her hands in her lap and sat straight and stiff, avoiding his gaze. He pulled away from the curb and headed down D Street. After turning onto Fifth, he glanced her way. She looked every bit as uncomfortable as she had when she climbed into the truck. Unfortunately, it was going to take a lot more than a four-block drive for her to let go of her uneasiness and relax with him.

As he turned into her driveway, his headlights swept across the front of the darkened house. A porch spanned its length, with a window on each side of the door, dressed with sheer curtains.

He tensed, all his senses on high alert. Did he just see movement inside?

Meagan reached for the door handle. "Thanks for—"

He held up a palm, eyes glued to the window. Beyond the curtains was a living room area. A wall at the back separated it from what was probably the kitchen. Had someone slipped behind that wall, startled by the truck's headlights?

"What is it?" It was just three words, spoken in the softest whisper, but fear permeated each one.

Before he could answer, a crouched figure darted from behind the wall and disappeared out the back door. Judging from Meagan's gasp, she saw it, too.

He turned off the engine, jumped out and pocketed the keys. "Stay here, and keep the truck locked."

When he rounded the rear of the house, no one was there. He hesitated only a moment, eyes straining in the darkness. A fence bordered the back, the boundary of the yard behind Meagan's. A hedge separated her property from the one next door. He charged off in that direction.

No one was in that yard, either. He sprinted along the hedge toward the street, then into a couple more yards. Finally, he admitted defeat and jogged back toward his truck. Another series of streaks lit up the sky, and thunder rumbled. But the storm seemed to be moving away. It might bypass them altogether.

As he approached his truck, apprehension shot through him. Meagan was gone. His gaze shot to the darkened house. If she had gone inside, she would have turned on the lights. Had the intruder circled around and forced her from the truck?

"Meagan?" No answer. He called her name again, louder and sharper.

Something moved in his peripheral vision, and he

snapped his head around in time to see her rise inside the truck. He almost crumpled in relief. She had apparently been crouched on the floorboard, hiding.

He tapped on the window. She was in the seat now, eyes wide. Since she didn't appear anywhere near ready to unlock the door, he used the key.

"I'm sorry. He got away."

She nodded, but made no move to get out. Her green eyes were still wide, her face pasty in the shadows inside the truck. She looked so vulnerable, it kicked his protective instincts into overdrive.

"I'm going to call for help. Then we'll go in together. Okay?"

She nodded again. She appeared stunned. Shell-shocked. She was hiding from someone. And terrified of being caught.

How long had it been? Just since coming to Cedar Key? Or had she lived other places, too, taking off whenever that someone got too close? Living like a nomad. Always looking over her shoulder. Never safe. Never at rest. He had to find a way to help her. But she would have to tell him what she was afraid of.

He made the call, then pocketed the phone. "The police are on the way. Let's go inside. I'll stay with you." He would bring her bike in later.

He took her hand to help her from the truck. But even after she was on her feet, he didn't release her. He led her toward the house, still keeping her hand in his. It just seemed the right thing to do.

When they had stepped onto the porch, she stopped and looked up at him. There was softness in her gaze, and it touched something deep inside him, something that had been dead for a long time.

He dropped her hand and squashed whatever it was that had just passed between them.

Four years ago, his life had been perfect. He'd been living in Ocala, surrounded by family and friends and engaged to Denise, his childhood sweetheart. Three weeks before their wedding date, she'd been on her way to meet the wedding planner when a drunk driver had crossed the line. Her life was over in an instant.

That was when he'd packed up and made a fresh start on Cedar Key. Now, four years later, time had taken the edge off the pain. Life wasn't perfect, but it was good. As long as he stayed busy.

Meagan attempted a shaky smile but didn't quite succeed. "Thanks. I'm glad you were here."

"Yeah. Me, too." If she'd been alone, she likely would have walked in on the intruder.

After she unlocked the door, he followed her inside. She flipped a switch, and soft yellow light chased the shadows from the room. It was sparsely furnished. A wooden desk sat in one corner with a lamp on top. A couch occupied part of another wall, with a coffee table in front of it. Across the room was a small stand with an even smaller television perched on top.

Most striking, though, was the total lack of personal belongings. There were no pictures, no knickknacks, nothing to make the space distinctly hers. Like a motel room.

Or the residence of someone who needed to travel light.

When he stepped into the kitchen, it didn't take long to figure out how the intruder had gained access. The French-style back door was open, the pane of glass next to the knob broken. A wrench lay on the stoop.

"Does that belong to you?" He angled his head that direction.

Her eyes widened. "No. Maybe he used it to break the window, then dropped it when he ran."

The doorbell rang, and a second later the front door swung inward. Bobby, the officer on duty, stood there.

Hunter filled him in on everything that had happened. "We know how the intruder gained access, but we don't know why." He turned to Meagan. "Anything missing?"

She disappeared into her bedroom, then reappeared moments later. Apparently that room was as sparsely furnished as the living room. "Not that I can tell."

Bobby addressed her. "I'm going to try to lift some prints. I'll dust the door, the knob and the wrench. Anything else look like it's been disturbed?"

Meagan didn't respond. She was standing in the center of the kitchen, brows drawn together.

Hunter stepped closer. "What's wrong?"

"The stove is crooked. Maybe it's been like that, but I've never noticed it before."

"I'll dust that, too." Bobby turned to leave the room.

Her eyes grew wide, and she drew in a sharp breath. "No, no fingerprints."

Bobby turned back around, brows raised in question.

Meagan continued. "I mean, it makes such a mess. I'm sure whoever came in was wearing gloves."

Bobby frowned. "We might have a burglar loose in Cedar Key. This is our chance to catch him before he breaks into any other houses."

"It's just so messy." Her voice had lost its fire.

"Not really," Bobby argued. "It's not that difficult to clean up, especially from hard surfaces. I'm going to go get my kit, and I'll be finished in no time."

As he disappeared out the front door, Meagan's shoulders slouched in resignation. Hunter studied her. Why didn't she want prints lifted? Was she really concerned about the mess? Or was she afraid they would find a match—to her?

Meagan's gaze shifted back to the stove. Her lower lip was trapped between her teeth, and vertical lines of worry marked the space between her brows. The stove was freestanding, gas, probably supplied by a propane tank outside. Had someone planned to tamper with it, to booby-trap it in some way to cause a fire?

Maybe the wrench had a dual purpose.

"Any idea who's behind all this?"

Meagan shook her head but didn't meet his eyes.

"Someone took a big chance coming in here when you were just riding to The Market and back."

"Maybe he thought I was going out for the evening."

"Or maybe his intent was to be waiting inside the house when you got home."

Her tight jaw and the determination in her eyes told him that was something she had already considered. And was trying hard not to think about.

He stepped closer and rested a hand on her shoulder. "Tell me what you're hiding from, Meagan."

Fear filled her eyes—just as when she had faced the reporters. And when she'd thought he might have overheard her conversation with Anna. But she didn't respond.

"Tell me what's going on." He kept his tone soothing, nonthreatening. "Let me help you."

Her gaze dipped to her feet, and several more moments passed. Finally, she shook her head. Whatever secrets lay in her past, she was nowhere near ready to let him in.

His chest tightened, his desire to protect her warring

with her determination to hold on to her secrets. If only she would talk. If she was running from some psycho ex-boyfriend, she could have the whole Cedar Key Police Department watching out for her.

And one officer in particular staying especially close. Because those haunted green eyes weren't going to let him do otherwise.

That had to be her story—she was running from a psycho ex-boyfriend. But there was another possibility, one he didn't want to consider—that she might be running from the law. Though the thought had lodged itself somewhere in the back of his mind, it was too much at odds with what little he had seen of Meagan. She couldn't be a fugitive. She seemed too sweet. Too pure.

But so did a lot of con artists.

Ever since arriving in Cedar Key, Meagan had kept to herself. She went to and from her job at Darci's Collectibles and Gifts and, every few days, took out that little boat of hers. But any invitations to social activities she politely turned down.

Maybe it was time to get to know her, beyond occasional casual greetings. Maybe she needed his help.

But if the opposite was true, and she was running from a criminal past, he would do what he had to do. He would bring her to justice. It was his job.

No matter how sweet and innocent she seemed.

TWO

The air was chilly and damp, the darkness complete. Meagan felt her way along the narrow passage, palms turned outward, the stone floor cold and rough beneath the soles of her feet. Why was she barefoot? Where did she leave her shoes?

She crossed her arms over her stomach, clutching the fabric at her sides. Silk. She wasn't only barefoot, she was also dressed in her nightgown. Its thin spaghetti straps and short length offered little covering, which further amplified her sense of vulnerability.

She continued down the passageway, touching the walls only enough to stay in the center of the path. Sticky strands fell across her face and neck, and a startled shriek shot up her throat.

Spiderwebs.

She stamped and spun, clawing at her face, running her fingers through her hair and brushing her hands down her front in a frantic, spastic dance.

Spiders. There were spiders in the passageway. Something passed over her bare foot, featherlight, and another scream made its way up her throat. She stumbled forward at a half run. Spiders were everywhere—crunching beneath her feet as she ran and falling into her hair.

Suddenly, the ground dropped from beneath her and she fell, landing with a splash in a lake. The water folded over her, her momentum propelling her deeper. She was going to drown. She had escaped the spiders but was going to drown.

No. She wasn't a six-year-old child anymore, sinking beneath the surface for the final time. She was a determined adult who had learned how to swim, who had spent months conquering her fear of the water.

With strong kicks and smooth strokes, she propelled herself upward. Moments later, she burst through the surface and sucked in huge gulps of air, eyes still squeezed shut.

A hand clamped around her throat.

Her eyes snapped open.

Edmund.

She sprang upright in bed with a gasp, nightgown drenched with perspiration and heart racing. Since escaping Edmund, she was no stranger to nightmares. But this one was the granddaddy of them all, preying on every one of her fears. Well, not *every* one. There were no snakes.

Edmund's mistake had been falling in love with an illusion. Every night, he had come alone to the restaurant where she'd worked, and she had waited on him. The waitress persona had been sweet and compliant, taking care of his every need. Unfortunately, he hadn't been able to see past the facade to the strong, determined woman beneath—a woman who had begun working at age sixteen, to help support her younger sister and give her opportunities she herself never had. Who had waitressed nights and weekends and gone to school days to improve her own lot in life.

When he realized he hadn't gotten the woman he thought he had, he'd vowed to break her.

He almost did.

Meagan climbed from bed, grabbed her robe and headed toward the door, determined to shake off the last remnants of the dream. Having someone break into her house had left her more jittery than normal. Even though Hunter had nailed a board over the broken pane, her security had been shattered along with the glass.

Running into Anna hadn't helped, either. Maybe it was coincidence, but when she'd described the "reporter" who had come in asking questions, she'd painted a perfect image of Lou, Edmund's butler.

Though Lou held the title, he wasn't a stuffy, proper Englishman walking around in a tux. He was more like a bodyguard, a tough New Yorker right out of the Bronx, with the muscles and scar to match. Whoever had created that scar had likely fared far worse than Lou had.

Meagan glanced at the clock on her way out of the room. It was only three-thirty, but her night was over, at least as far as sleep was concerned. She would be better off picking up a book.

As she reached for the light switch, her gaze fell on the window near the desk. Behind the slits in the mini-blinds, a shadow passed by. She froze, arm extended. A cold knot of fear settled in her stomach. Had her intruder come back?

She dropped her hand and shut her eyes against the image that filled her mind—massive arms, a rock-hard chest, an inch-long scar marring one tanned cheek.

But Lou wouldn't hurt her. Not that he wouldn't be capable of it. He would just tell Edmund. Whatever Edmund had planned for her, he would want to carry out himself. And he would take pleasure in it.

She backed away from the switch, heart pounding out an erratic rhythm. Once she had retrieved her phone from the nightstand, she locked herself inside the bathroom and dialed 911. Then she sank to the edge of the tub. And for the five thousandth time in the past year, she wished she could somehow turn back the clock.

When she'd met Edmund, she hadn't been looking. She'd been focused on work and school and keeping her head above water. But Edmund had poured on the charm and swept her off her feet. He was so confident and powerful. Calm and in control of his emotions. The complete opposite of her abusive father.

Now she knew better. What she had seen as calm control was actually coldness at its extreme. A heart that had stopped feeling years ago.

A siren sounded in the distance, grew louder, then fell silent. Several more minutes passed before she found the nerve to step from the bathroom. When she swung open the front door, a police cruiser sat in her driveway. To her left, the beam of a flashlight shone from around the side of the house, and to her right, truck headlights moved toward her.

Moments later, Bobby appeared from the side of the house, flashlight in hand, and the truck eased to a stop. Hunter jumped out. What was *he* doing here? She cinched her robe more tightly.

Hunter's gaze swept her up and down. When his eyes locked on hers, they were filled with concern. He had offered to stay last night, to sleep on the couch. Maybe she shouldn't have been so quick to turn him down.

"I heard the siren and was afraid your intruder had come back. Are you all right?"

"I saw someone move past the window."

Bobby interrupted their conversation. "You'd better look at this." His expression was grim, his tone ominous.

Dread trickled over her. She hurried, barefoot, down the steps and around the side of the house, Hunter close on her heels.

"What is it?"

Instead of answering, Bobby raised the flashlight. Her heart dropped into her stomach, and her knees almost buckled. Painted in red, twelve-inch-tall capital letters was the word *MURDERER*. The letters stretched across the span of siding between her bedroom and living room windows, sloppy, painted in a hurry, but quite legible. Rivulets trailed from each letter. Like blood.

Meagan crossed her arms over her stomach, steeling herself against the nausea churning there. Her past had followed her to Cedar Key. Someone in California had found her.

Or someone in Cedar Key knew who she really was.

"Meagan?"

Hunter's voice penetrated her spinning thoughts. She lifted her gaze to his face. The tenderness that was usually there was gone. His jaw was set in a firm line, and his blue eyes held suspicion.

"What is this about?"

Even his tone was harsh. However this turned out, he wouldn't cut her any slack. No matter how gentle and caring he had seemed previously.

"I—I don't know."

Bobby turned to go. "I'm getting my camera."

Hunter stayed. He put his hands on his hips, his expression even more harsh, if that was possible. "Someone just painted *murderer* on your house. That's not a childish prank. Tell us what's going on."

"I don't know." This time she managed to put more strength behind the words. "I'm not a killer."

Even though she'd been one of only two people in the house when Edmund's gardener was murdered. Even though her fingerprints were all over the murder weapon. Even though the blow had been delivered by someone left-handed.

The charges against her were dropped. There was no motive. And the investigators didn't believe she had the strength to do that kind of damage to Charlie's skull, even with a heavy brass candlestick.

She hadn't been able to help much with the investigation. All she knew at the time was that Charlie owed someone money. And that she didn't kill him.

Then she'd found out who had. And she'd disappeared.

Hunter took two steps toward her, his stance intimidating. "Give me one reason I should believe you. You're obviously running from something. I'd hoped it was a psycho ex-boyfriend. But this doesn't look good."

"I've never killed anyone."

Hunter didn't respond, just studied her for several moments. He was standing close, invading her personal space. But she refused to step back. Or squirm under his intense scrutiny.

Bobby returned with a camera and began snapping pictures while he talked. "Any idea who did this?"

She faced him, giving Hunter a stiff shoulder. Bobby was the officer on duty. She would direct her answers to him.

"I have no idea." And that was the truth. If someone was blaming her for Charlie's death, why wait till now? There had been plenty of opportunity to threaten her earlier. After Charlie was killed, she'd spent another two months in Edmund's house.

Bobby snapped another photo, the flash blinding in the darkness. "Do you think this incident and someone breaking into your house earlier tonight are related?"

"Possibly. But I don't see the connection."

"I'm going to look around. The grass is too thick right here, but I'd like to see if the person left behind any footprints. I'm also going to take some samples of the paint."

A spark of hope lit the despair that had fallen over her. Maybe they would be able to tell where it came from and who'd purchased it.

Her gaze shifted back to the wall. The letters were barely visible in the dim glow of a nearby streetlight— dark, ugly stains against the white siding. "Can I wash this off as soon as you're finished?" Since it was brushed instead of spray painted, maybe it would scrub clean.

"Sure."

Hunter followed Bobby around front, and Meagan breathed a sigh of relief. Maybe he was done grilling her. Bobby came across as an investigator seeking the answers he needed to solve the case. Hunter's questions held an undertone of accusation.

Instead of leaving, he reappeared a minute later with a flashlight, ready to help Bobby with the investigation. Fine. She would go inside and leave them to their work.

A short time later there was a soft knock on her front door. Both officers stood on her porch. "We're finished now." It was Bobby who spoke.

"Thanks. I'll get that paint washed off."

When she bade them good-night, Bobby took the cue and left. Hunter didn't.

"Do you have a scrub brush? I'll help you clean that up."

"Thanks, but I've got it."

Stubbornness crept into his features. "I'm not leaving until you're locked safely back inside. So you may as well let me help you."

As she stepped out the door with a bucket, some dish soap and a brush, relief nudged some of the annoyance aside. With a prowler on the loose, standing outside alone in the middle of the night wasn't the smartest thing to do. It was almost worth the suspicious glances and prying questions to have Hunter's protection.

But over the next ten minutes, there weren't any suspicious glances *or* prying questions. He insisted on doing the scrubbing and had her hold the hose. The paint seemed to come off well, with little, if any, tint remaining behind. The real test would be when the sun came up.

He walked her to the front door. "Keep everything locked. And call if anything at all seems off. I'll give you my cell number."

"That's okay. If it's an emergency, I'll just call 911. I don't want to bother you."

"It's no bother. It's my job."

"Not when you're off duty."

He started to turn, then hesitated. "Don't leave Cedar Key." It wasn't a request. It was a command.

"Don't worry. I won't." She had no choice. As much as she longed to run, that wasn't an option. Her funds were too low. The bus ticket from California had taken a good chunk of what she had squirreled away. And getting set up in the small house she rented had taken most of the rest. By the time Darci had given her the part-time job in her gift shop, Meagan hadn't been sure how she was going to eat the following week.

No, she would have to save up much more than a measly four hundred dollars before she was ready to disappear again. Until then, she was stuck. Regardless of who might be stalking her.

She watched Hunter step off the porch, then closed and locked the door. For some reason, the emptiness of the house seemed more pronounced than ever, mirroring the emptiness of her life.

Instead of returning to bed, she opened the desk drawer and removed two paperbacks she had picked up at a garage sale last weekend. A third book lay underneath. It was old—a small, thick book of classic poetry—and one of the few things she had brought with her from California. It had belonged to Charlie. She had borrowed it so many times, he had joked that he would will it to her when he died.

That day came sooner than either of them had anticipated.

But the books weren't what she was after. The drawer held one other cherished item—a five-by-seven photo. It was the only one she had. She'd left all the albums behind, with their pictures of family camping trips, picnics, her sister's roller-hockey tournaments. She'd had no choice. If one had been missing, Edmund would have known the truth.

So she had settled for a single photo, hidden years ago when a more current one was put into the frame in front of it. It was of the three of them—her mom, her sister and her. Meagan had been twelve at the time, her sister only six. Ever since their dad went to jail for the last time and their mom became both mother and father, the three of them had been inseparable. Until Edmund.

One of his first steps in taking over her life had been talking her into quitting school. Not permanently. Just one semester. A break to focus all her attention on getting her art career off the ground. If she would move into his house, she could give up her waitressing job and do nothing but paint.

And her clunker of a car that needed work—why dump money into it when his butler would chauffeur her anywhere she wanted to go in the Mercedes? Each choice had seemed like a no-brainer. Trading a small apartment downtown for a mansion on twenty acres. A 1992 Pontiac Sunbird for a brand-new Mercedes. Hours on her feet serving demanding customers for days spent painting in a large, sunny studio overlooking the lake.

What she hadn't recognized until much too late was that the real trade she had made was freedom for bondage.

She removed the picture from the bottom of the drawer, the longing in her heart threatening to tear it in two. So many times she had picked up the phone and dialed her mother's number, but never hit Send. Her mom and sister lived less than twenty miles from Edmund. There was always that slim chance their paths could cross. And if they knew she was alive, Edmund would see their happiness and pry the reason out of them somehow.

So she would never do more than dial the number. And stare at a twelve-year-old photo.

When she boarded the bus for Florida, she'd thought she had gained her freedom. She was wrong.

She was no longer living under Edmund's roof, but he still invaded her dreams.

He had no more control over her friendships, but she could never let anyone get close.

She wasn't a victim of his mind games anymore, but

she lived with the constant fear that he would one day find her.

No, she wasn't free.

Freedom was nothing but an illusion.

Hunter eased his cruiser to a stop in front of Darci's Collectibles and Gifts. The older red Corolla was parked at the curb, which meant Darci was there. So was the pink Schwinn bike, Meagan's mode of transportation.

When he entered the store, Darci stood at the counter unpacking a small box of office supplies. She looked up from her work to offer him a vibrant smile. "What are you up to?"

"Just the usual. Hanging out, keeping the streets of Cedar Key crime-free." Investigating a suspicious woman with "murderer" painted on the side of her house.

He glanced around the shop. Meagan was nowhere to be seen. She was probably avoiding him. For good reason. She was hiding something. At least she wasn't a flight risk, not on a bicycle. Or in a johnboat powered by a four-horse motor.

Darci pulled a pack of fluorescent-colored Post-It notes from the box and set them beside the pens and calculator tape already on the counter. "It's been busy today. We've finally hit a lull, but we've had a steady stream of customers all morning."

Before he could respond, the phone began to ring, drawing Meagan out of hiding. She slipped past Darci and laid an envelope on the counter, avoiding eye contact with him. Yep, definitely someone with something to hide.

As soon as he could get Darci alone, he'd talk to her. If she would give him the information he needed, he'd put it through the database. Running the numbers on

Meagan's boat registration sticker had led nowhere. They
were easy enough to get; she kept the boat pulled up on
the narrow strip of beach at Darci's parents' place. But
it was still in Darci's dad's name. And Meagan had no
car tag to run. According to Darci, she didn't even have
a bank account. She cashed her checks at Darci's bank,
then paid her bills with cash or money orders.

Meagan picked up the envelope she had previously
laid down and began to tap it against the counter. Whoever was on the phone was apparently trying to sell
her something, judging from her side of the conversation. But Meagan wasn't budging. Finally, she hung up.
Whether the conversation actually ended or she got fed
up and cut it short, he couldn't tell.

She handed the envelope to Darci.

"What's this?"

Meagan shrugged. "I don't know. I assumed it was
yours. I found it on a shelf in the back where the beach-
themed stuff is."

Darci broke the seal and removed a single sheet of
paper. As soon as she unfolded it, her eyes widened and
her brows drew together.

Meagan stepped closer, and her gaze dipped to the
page. Her reaction was stronger than Darci's. She gasped
and stumbled backward, her hand to her chest.

"What is it?" He couldn't see what was written from
his position across the counter.

Darci handed him what she held. Three lines of
slanted black print filled the center of the page: *You
killed him. For this you will die.*

Darci shook her head. "I'm sure it wasn't there when I
straightened up yesterday. So that means someone left it
today. But I have no idea who. Probably a couple dozen
people came through here this morning."

"Is there anything in particular that you can remember about any of them? Anything out of the ordinary? Anyone acting strange?"

"Not that I recall. They all just seemed like normal tourists to me. Meagan?"

Meagan swallowed hard and shook her head. She hadn't said a word since Darci opened the letter. She *had* managed to make it to a stool, though, which was a good thing. As pale as she had gotten, Hunter wasn't sure she would be able to stand on her own. A pang of tenderness shot through him. Regardless of what she had done, the fear and vulnerability in her eyes wove their way straight to his heart. But he wouldn't let that get in the way of doing his job.

"Were any of your visitors big guys with close-cropped hair and a scar on one cheek?" He kept his eyes on Darci, trying to ignore Meagan's glare. Yes, he'd been eavesdropping, and now she knew.

Darci raised her brows. "It sounds as if you're thinking of someone in particular."

"A guy was in Nature's Landing yesterday asking a lot of questions about Meagan."

"What makes you think this has anything to do with Meagan? The note wasn't addressed to anyone."

"Just a wild guess." He cast a glance at Meagan. She obviously hadn't said anything to Darci about her early-morning discovery. "And the fact that someone painted *murderer* on the side of her house this morning."

Now it was Darci's turn to gasp. "Why?"

"That's what I'm hoping she'll tell us, especially since this someone is making some pretty serious threats."

Meagan squared her shoulders and straightened her spine. "I don't know who's doing this. I've never killed anybody." Some of the color was returning to her face, and her voice held some strength now. There was also a flash of defiance in her eyes that hadn't been there a few moments ago. "Someone is targeting the wrong person."

Hunter studied her. She seemed to be telling the truth, but he couldn't say for sure. People who were good at lying could do it without flinching. His twin brother was a prime example. He had lied all his life, at least since he was old enough to talk. He lied even when it was easier to tell the truth.

Maybe Meagan didn't kill anyone. But there was a whole lot that she wasn't telling them. Now that someone was threatening her life, he needed to learn the details of her past and what had brought her to Cedar Key. But Meagan wasn't talking.

She glanced at the sailboat clock hanging behind the counter. "I've got five more minutes, so I'll finish what I was working on when the phone rang, then head out."

"I need to do a police report." He looked down at the page he still held. "And I'll take this in as evidence." Unfortunately, any prints were likely destroyed. But he would give it a shot.

By the time he had asked Meagan a few questions, her shift was over. Worry tightened his chest at the thought of her riding home alone. "Let me take you. Your bike should fit in the trunk." It might not close, but her house was only a few blocks away.

"That's okay. At two o'clock in the afternoon, no one is likely to bother me."

He nodded and bade the two women farewell. Meagan wouldn't let him take her home. But she couldn't stop him from following at a distance. After making a large circle of a couple blocks, he rounded the corner onto Second Street as Meagan walked from the store. With her back to him, she got on her bike and began to pedal down the street. Once he saw her safely home, he would go back and talk to Darci.

When he stepped into the store ten minutes later, two customers were leaving. Darci looked at him with raised brows.

"You're back."

A quick glance around told him they were alone. Hopefully, it would stay that way, at least for a few minutes. "Yeah. I need to talk to you about Meagan. What do you know about her?" He and Darci had been friends long enough that he didn't have to waste time with small talk.

"Well, she said she moved from a little town in Indiana. I can't even remember the name of it now. She doesn't talk about her prior life much. In fact, she doesn't talk about it at all."

"Don't you find that odd? I mean, you've worked together for what, five weeks now? Six?"

"Coming up on six."

"When women spend that much time together, don't they usually share stories and stuff?"

Darci rested her hand on a pack of Post-It notes and slid her thumb up the edge, fanning through them. "Not necessarily."

"Okay, how much does she know about you?"

"That's different. I'm a really open person." She grinned at him. "And I talk a lot."

"I won't argue with that."

"You don't have to agree so readily." She threw the Post-Its at him.

He caught them in midair and laid them back on the counter. "Seriously, how much do you know about her, other than that she came from a small town in Indiana?"

"She has a sister."

"Older? Younger?"

"Younger."

"Parents?"

"Mom. She never mentioned a father. But she doesn't have contact anymore with her mom or sister."

"Why not?"

"I don't know. She was clearly uncomfortable, so I didn't ask." She crossed her arms and gave him an accusatory glare. "Some people don't like to pry. The only reason I know about her no longer having contact with her mom and sister was because she didn't have any family members she could put down on the emergency contact form I had her fill out."

"So what else do you know about her?"

"That's all I can think of right now."

"And you don't find that odd." Something didn't add up with Meagan Berry, despite Darci's lack of concern. Hunter had been a cop too long to share her trusting attitude. And he'd been conned too many times to take anything at face value.

"No, I don't. She went through some pretty traumatic stuff, and right now, she's just trying to forget."

"She told you that?"

"She didn't have to. Women can sense these things. She'll open up when she's ready."

That wasn't good enough. Whatever Darci "sensed," he wasn't willing to go on intuition. "Did you have a background check run on her before hiring her?"

She shook her head.

"If you were hiring someone you've known all your life, I can see skipping all that. But not a stranger who's being really secretive about who she is and where she came from. Don't you think a background check would be a good idea? I mean, she's handling your money."

Something flashed in Darci's eyes. "No, I trust my gut. And my gut tells me Meagan's not a criminal."

He didn't miss the defensiveness in her tone. "Look, I'm not saying she's an ax murderer or anything. But she was totally freaked out about having her picture taken. That's a sure sign of someone who's hiding something."

"Maybe she just doesn't like to be in the spotlight. She's a private person."

"It's more than that. She just had *murderer* painted on the side of her house. And now someone is threatening to kill her."

With his last statement, some of the stubbornness left Darci's eyes. Maybe she was weakening. He leaned against the counter, which put him a little closer to her. "Let me check her out, just to be on the safe side. You have her Social Security number and date of birth, right?"

"Of course I do. But I'm not giving them to you." She dug in her heels, five foot three inches of stubborn determination. "That's confidential information."

"Come on, Darci. I need to do this. You have to admit she's hiding something. And I owe it to the people of Cedar Key to find out what."

"Then get a warrant. Or a subpoena." She planted both hands on her hips. "Don't you have police work you need to do?"

"This *is* police work." Hunter sighed. He was getting nowhere. Darci was sticking up for Meagan as if she were her oldest childhood friend. "Look, you're sure she's not hiding from the law. But she's hiding from something. We'll have a much better chance of helping her if we can find out what she's running from."

He paused, then continued, his tone pleading. "She's scared, Darci."

She studied him for several moments. Then recognition dawned in her eyes, and a slow smile climbed up her cheeks. "You like her, don't you?"

"Of course I do. She's a nice lady."

"No, I mean you *like* her. Finally, there's someone capable of cracking the armor of the untouchable Hunter Kingston."

"That imagination of yours is working overtime again. I'm concerned for Meagan the same way I'm concerned about every resident of Cedar Key."

"Uh-huh."

Uh-huh, nothing. Darci didn't know what she was talking about. Meagan was cute. And she seemed sweet. In fact, she had intrigued him from the moment she first showed up in Cedar Key. Her incredible artistic ability, that shy smile, those expressive green eyes... But he wasn't looking.

If he was, he would look for someone with integrity, someone he could trust. Not someone with a dark past, surrounded by a web of lies. He'd been lied to all his life. Conned and stolen from. The last thing he needed was more deceit.

He pushed the dark thoughts aside. "So are you going to help me or not?"

"I already told you, that information's confidential. I'm not allowed to give it to anyone without Meagan's permission."

"No problem."

He would find out what he needed to know with or without her help. Bobby had been able to get several viable prints from her place last night. They had already been turned over to Levy County to process. Anytime now they would get the results back.

Something told him there were some surprises in store.

THREE

Dark clouds rolled across the sky, and thunder rumbled in the distance. Meagan pedaled harder, struggling against the wind. She would be hard-pressed to make it home before the sky opened up. One of the drawbacks to getting places on a bicycle during a Florida summer.

She made a left from D Street onto Fifth. One more block. An engine revved behind her, probably someone who had also just made a turn. But instead of backing off, the driver continued to accelerate. She cast a worried glance over her left shoulder. A white sedan sped down the road toward her.

She was used to sharing the streets of Cedar Key with vehicles—slow-moving ones. From trucks and SUVs all the way down to golf carts. Lots of golf carts. She had gotten over her nervousness at riding in the street weeks ago. But getting that note yesterday changed everything.

Besides, the sedan wasn't moving slowly. It was already going faster than it should for the residential neighborhood and was continuing to accelerate. It wasn't weaving, moving erratically or threatening in any other way, except for the speed. But she wasn't taking chances. She eased to the edge of the road, ready to veer off if need be, and cast another glance over her shoulder. The car suddenly angled straight toward her.

A bolt of panic shot through her. She jerked the handlebars to the right, desperate to get away from the three thousand pounds of metal bearing down on her. Her front wheel hit sand where the grass was sparse, and jerked the handlebars farther right, while the back wheel twisted left.

Meagan went airborne. Everything happened so fast, she didn't have time to react. She landed with a grunt on her left shoulder and hip, and rolled. How many times, she didn't know. A crunch of metal registered through her panic, and she came to a stop against the rough bark of a tree. A root protruded from the ground under her left hip, which was likely already bruised from the fall.

Tires squealed, and she pushed herself to a seated position in time to see the sedan turn the corner. Then it was gone. Along with the dim hope she had held on to that the message on the side of her house and the note were nothing more than a twisted prank.

Someone was trying to kill her. And she had no idea who.

Edmund didn't own a white sedan. Of course, it could be a rental car. In fact, if he wanted to run her over, he wouldn't use his own vehicle.

But somehow, that didn't sound like Edmund. When he finally found her, he would try to kill her. She had no doubt. But he would do it with his own hands, close enough to look her in the eye and see her regret, smell her fear.

She eased herself to her feet, testing her limbs as she stood. Her knees and ankles were okay. So was her spine. Except for a bruised hip and some tenderness in her left shoulder, she was fine.

She reached into her pocket to get her phone. She needed to call 911. There was only one way on and off Cedar Key. If they set up a roadblock on Highway 24, maybe they could apprehend the driver.

If not, she wouldn't be much help. She wasn't able to get the tag number. She didn't get a look at the driver, either. The windows were too tinted. And she'd been too focused on trying to get out of the path of the car to zero in on details.

Her eyes dropped to her phone, and her heart fell. The screen was shattered, with multicolored blotches and streaks running behind the jagged lines. She needed to borrow a phone. She took two quick steps toward her bike, then stopped. It hadn't fared any better than her phone had. It lay on the ground ten feet away, frame bent, wheels crushed.

A strong gust swept through and whipped the ends of her hair against her cheeks. The sky burst open, pouring rain over her. Leaving her bike, she sprinted to the nearest house with a car in the driveway. Old Mrs. Tackett was always home.

Within minutes, help was on its way. That help came in the form of Hunter. Meagan waved from Mrs. Tackett's porch, and he pulled into the driveway. She would have preferred Bobby, but at the moment she would take anybody.

From everything she had seen of Hunter, he was a good cop. He just made her uneasy, always pushing for information she would never be able to share.

The door of the cruiser swung open. A black umbrella appeared first, then Hunter stepped out. She met him at the car. She was drenched, with drops of water falling from her bangs into her eyes. But Mrs. Tackett had pressed an umbrella into her hand and insisted that she keep it. She would return it later.

Hunter's eyes were filled with concern. "Are you hurt?"

"No, just a little bruised." And a lot shaken up.

"We've already got a BOLO out with Levy County on the white sedan. Since your bike is pretty mangled, there's probably damage to the car. Anything else you can tell me?"

"No. I was so focused on staying alive, I missed everything else. The description I gave the dispatcher is pretty much it."

Which was pretty much nothing. White sedan, tinted windows. And now probably some good dents and scratches on the right front bumper. Maybe some pink paint.

She crossed the street and led him two doors down, to where her bike lay in the grass.

Hunter frowned. "If they left any tire tracks, this storm has pretty well washed them away."

He was right. Already water had collected at the edge of the road and was running downhill in a steady stream. And the deluge didn't look to be letting up anytime soon.

Hunter continued. "We're searching Cedar Key, and Levy County is setting up a roadblock at the marshes between the Number Four Channel Bridge and Cedar Key Plantation to catch anyone trying to leave."

His eyes shifted to the mangled bike and then back to her face. Anger had pushed aside some of the concern. "You could have been killed."

"I think that was the point." There was no sense in trying to deny it. After yesterday's note, she couldn't pass it off as coincidence.

He asked her several more questions, most of which

she wasn't able to answer, and had her relay step by step what had happened from the time she turned onto Fifth until the car sped out of sight. After that, he took several pictures. Finally, he picked up the bike and loaded it into the trunk of his cruiser.

"Get in and I'll take you home."

"That's not necessary. It's a few doors down."

Even as she said the words, she knew there would be no deterring him. There was a steely determination in his blue eyes.

"Come on, Meagan, it's pouring rain."

"I'm soaked. I'll get your seat wet."

"It'll dry."

She shrugged and stepped into the car. As long as he didn't press her for answers. Because she really didn't have any. Nothing that had happened this afternoon fit Edmund at all. And the chance that some friend or relative of Charlie's was coming after her in Cedar Key just didn't compute.

When Hunter got in, he turned the key in the ignition. But instead of pulling away from the curb, he looked over at her. The determination in his eyes was tempered with concern. "Someone just tried to kill you. Don't you think it's time to level with me?"

"I can't tell you what I don't know."

"You know more than you're letting on. Tell me, Meagan." His tone had softened. It was now gentle and pleading. "What are you running from? Who is after you?"

She closed her eyes and tried to still her pounding heart. Rain beat against the roof, but she was safe and protected inside her metal cocoon, Hunter next to her. His calming presence filled the car, and his masculine scent wrapped around her, woodsy with a hint of spice.

She inhaled slowly, drawing it all in—his strength, his gentleness, his concern.

Her throat tightened, and her determination crumbled, leaving her with an overwhelming urge to throw everything she had held on to for the past several months at Hunter's feet. She was tired. Tired of running. Tired of the fear. And so tired of being alone. She longed to rest and let someone else take care of everything. Just for a little while.

She let her head fall back against the seat, and stared through the windshield. The wiper blades swished across the glass, providing brief moments of clarity through the river distorting the view ahead.

Clarity. What she wouldn't give for some of that right now. A clear path to follow. Knowing whether to run or stay. Knowing who to trust.

She lifted her head. Certainly not Hunter.

She had faked her own death. If that wasn't illegal, falsifying information on her I-9 and other employment documents was. And Hunter was a cop. An honest one. He'd have to turn her in.

Then it would be all over. Edmund would know she was alive, and there would be nowhere to run. Because he would follow every lead, turn over every rock. With his acres of vineyards and successful winery, he had the resources to do it. And if his own millions somehow fell short, there was always his family's expansive estate in Italy. For Edmund, money was no object. He would do whatever necessary to find her.

Then he would kill her.

It wouldn't be the first time he had killed someone. Or the second. She didn't have proof, but she had a dead man's blackmail letter. And a strong gut feeling.

Meagan shook her head. Hunter wanted to know who was after her, but she didn't know.

He sighed, then pulled away from the curb. When he came to a stop in her driveway, he didn't turn off the engine. "I'm calling the station before we go in."

"We?"

He ignored the question. "I want to know if they've found this white sedan."

When he finished the call, his face was grim. "There's been no sign of it. It didn't head up 24." He opened the door and started to get out.

"What are you doing?"

"Seeing you safely inside." He hesitated. "You have a cell phone, right?"

"I did until a half hour ago. I landed on it when I fell, shattered the screen."

He frowned. "Do you have a landline?"

"No."

He closed the door and began to back from the driveway.

"What are you doing?"

"Getting you a new phone." He backed out onto Fifth, then glanced over at her. Some of the hardness had left his eyes. "I'm not leaving you alone here with no way to call out."

Warmth filled her chest, along with an odd sense of longing that seemed to come out of nowhere. He was suspicious of her, but he still refused to leave her cut off and unprotected. It had been a long time since someone had cared for her like that.

She pushed aside the thought and shored up her defenses. She had escaped Edmund and stayed alive the past two and a half months by being strong. And depending on nobody but herself. Sure, Hunter was good-looking and sweet and caring, but now wasn't the time to go all weak. Or let a man once again try to take over her life.

She opened her mouth to object, then snapped it shut again. Hunter was right. She needed a phone. And fighting him on it was not only senseless, but stupid. When she went to bed tonight, her new phone would be on her nightstand within easy reach.

Both Cedar Key and Levy County were looking for the white sedan. And no one had spotted it.

Which meant only one thing—whoever had tried to kill her was still on Cedar Key.

Hunter stood inside Darci's Collectibles and Gifts, leaning against the metal doorjamb. It was five minutes to six, and Meagan was there alone, closing out the day's business.

Since yesterday's attempt on her life, she'd been without a bike. Darci had taken her to work this morning, and he was giving her a ride home. Neither of them was willing to let her walk. Hunter wasn't willing to let her ride, either. Once she got a new bike, he would probably have a battle on his hands.

She rounded the corner and met him at the door with a half smile. "Thanks."

He nodded. As long as he wasn't pressing her for information, she was amicable—not exactly warm, but not bristly, either.

That was soon to change.

They had a match on the prints, and there were surprises. Big ones.

He opened the passenger door for her and helped her in. When he slid into the driver's seat, she was staring out the windshield, her dark hair falling in soft waves around her face. He wasn't sure what the natural color was. When she had first arrived in Cedar Key, it was deep black. Now it was a rich brown, like his mother's antique walnut desk, catching the light with hints of red. Though still short, it had grown out quite a bit in the past two or three months. Soft and relaxed, with just the right amount of natural wave, the longer style suited her better.

He eased from the parallel parking space in front of the store and went around the block to head toward the small house on Fifth Street.

She released a soft sigh. "I'm sorry about this."

He glanced over to find her watching him. "What?"

"You having to pick me up. I'll work on getting a new bike this weekend."

He pulled into her driveway and turned off the truck. "Under the circumstances, I'd rather drive you."

Instead of responding, she just stared at him, her usually expressive eyes unreadable. Emotion swam somewhere near the surface, hidden behind the air of aloofness that had surrounded her from the moment she'd arrived in Cedar Key.

"I'll manage. It's not your responsibility to take care of me. Not even in your position as a Cedar Key police officer."

"It's my responsibility to protect all of my citizens." And that was why he was going to do what he had to do. "I need to talk to you. Is it all right if we go inside?"

She stiffened, and fear flashed in her green eyes. He could almost see the walls around her strengthen. She hesitated a moment longer, then squared her shoulders and gave a brief dip of her head.

Once inside, she eased down onto the couch. But she didn't lean back. Instead she sat straight and stiff, hands folded in her lap. He chose the recliner adjacent to her.

"You know the prints we lifted? Levy ran them through the FBI database."

"Really?" Her voice was a couple pitches higher than normal. "Any matches?"

"Yeah. They all belong to an Elaina Thomas."

Her eyebrows lifted in question, a facade of nonchalance layered thinly over panic. "You mean it was a woman who broke in?"

"That's how it appears. There's only one problem. Elaina Thomas died almost three months ago."

Her brows drew together, and she gave a couple of rapid blinks. "How—how is that possible?"

Anger flared in him. More lies. He was giving her a chance to come clean, but she was choosing to continue the deceit. Just like his brother.

"Don't play me, Meagan." He narrowed his gaze. "Or should I call you Elaina?"

Her eyes fell to her hands. They were still folded, but clenched so tightly her fingers were discolored. Fear radiated from her. Suddenly she seemed small and fragile. And so alone.

Tenderness forged a path through the anger and burrowed deep in his heart. In that moment, she wasn't just a possible fugitive, living under an alias, hiding a dark and deceptive past. She was a woman, scared and vulnerable.

But he had to ask the hard questions. It was his job.

"Elaina Thomas was charged with first degree murder. Then the charges were dropped. What happened?"

"I didn't do it."

"Are you running from the circumstances surrounding that murder? Is that why you faked your death?"

She shook her head but otherwise didn't respond.

"Then tell me. Why did you run? Why did you go to the extremes that you did? What are you afraid of?"

He kept his tone soft and gentle. He couldn't be stern with her now if he tried. It would be like kicking a defenseless child.

So much time passed that he didn't think she would answer. Finally, she drew in a long, shaky breath and lifted her gaze to his face. Her eyes still held fear. But something else was there, too—determination.

She shook her head. "I can't."

"Did you commit a crime?" Not that she would tell him if she had. But maybe he would be able to sense if she was lying. "Are you running from the law?"

"No."

It was just a single word. But the conviction behind it blasted holes in the suspicions he had had since the moment someone had branded her a killer.

"Then what are you running from?" Or more likely, *who*?

She shook her head again. "I can't tell you. I can't tell anyone."

He leaned forward and lightly touched her jean-clad leg. "Tell me what you're afraid of. I can help."

"No." She crossed her arms in front of her, as if suddenly chilled. "No one can help."

"Meagan," he began, then stopped. That wasn't even her name. "You faked your death. You're living under an alias. What kind of a cop would I be if I just accepted your claim that you're not running from the law?"

"What are you saying?"

"I think you know what I'm saying. Give me one good reason to not haul you in."

Her eyes widened, and fear flashed in their depths. "I'm not a killer. I've never committed any kind of crime. I've never even had a speeding ticket." Her tone turned pleading. "Please believe me."

"I don't have that option. As an officer of the law, I can't just let this go. Tell me what you're running from."

She shook her head again, so adamantly her hair bounced against her cheeks. "He'll kill me."

"Who?"

"Edmund."

"Edmund who?"

"I can't tell you. If he ever finds out that I'm alive, he'll hunt me down. He won't rest until I'm dead."

Hunter leaned forward again and locked gazes with her, hoping she would see the sincerity in his eyes and let down her guard. "No, he won't. We'll protect you. But you have to let us know what we're protecting you from."

She sank her teeth into her lower lip while indecision flashed across her features. Seconds stretched into a half minute.

"Please tell me, Meagan. Let me help you. Who is Edmund?"

Finally, she straightened her spine and raised her chin, her decision apparently made. "I can't. It's not just me. He said if I ever left, he would kill my mother and sister, too."

Just what Hunter had suspected. Meagan was running from a psycho ex-boyfriend.

Or was the whole thing one big con? She had already been charged with murder, then managed to get out of it.

She seemed sincere, the fear in her eyes real. And he was usually a pretty good judge of character. But he really didn't know her. She'd been on Cedar Key for less than three months. And since she kept to herself, he had spent very little time with her, none in a social setting. Would he even recognize a lie from her? Not if she was good.

Like his brother. He seemed to have been born with

the ability to lie. And steal and cheat and deceive. And somehow still come out on top. Those laughing blue eyes and that smooth, easy manner had kept him out of a lot of trouble. Then the charm had run out. Instead of a slap on the wrist, he'd gotten fifteen years.

Was it possible Meagan was a con artist, too? That risk wasn't his to take. He gave it one last shot.

"We can protect you."

She crossed her arms, her jaw set. "No."

He rose to his feet with a sigh. He had tried to get her to level with him, but gentle prying was getting him nowhere. What he was about to do would put a permanent rift between them. But she was leaving him no choice.

"Fine. We'll play it your way."

"Where are you going?"

"To get a warrant."

"For what?"

"All employment records for Darci's Collectibles and Gifts. I'm guessing we'll find a falsified I-9. That's a federal offense."

Meagan's eyes widened and filled with panic. But she still didn't speak. He crossed the room and reached for the doorknob.

"Abelli."

He withdrew his hand. "What?"

"Abelli. Edmund's last name is Abelli."

He eased back into the recliner, relief surging through him. She was going to talk. But she wasn't happy about it. Her arms were still crossed in front of her, and she stared straight ahead, her jaw tight.

"Who is Edmund Abelli? A crazy ex-boyfriend?"

"Fiancé."

"You wanted to break things off, and he wouldn't let you leave?"

She nodded.

"Did you get a restraining order?"

She shook her head. "I tried." Her tone was flat, without emotion. "He caught me before I could even make it to the courthouse."

Hunter's gut tightened, and though he really didn't want to know, he asked the question, anyway. "What did he do?"

She turned her head until her eyes met his. "For the next week I could hardly walk."

The nonanswer told him everything he needed to know. He clenched his fists, trying to beat back the fury pumping through his veins. Not just crazy. Abusive. And Edmund had apparently gotten away with it.

Hunter drew in a slow, calming breath. "Did you go to the police?"

She shook her head. "He said he would do the same thing to my little sister, except worse. And I knew he would. He had ways of keeping me in line."

Meagan began to rock back and forth, her eyes squeezed shut against the memories assaulting her. His chest tightened, and the urge to draw her into his arms was almost overpowering. But it wasn't his place to offer comfort. He was a cop, and she was a suspect. There were distinct lines he couldn't cross.

He sprang to his feet. Forget professionalism. He eased onto the couch next to her and draped an arm across her shoulders. She tensed, but only for a moment.

"It's okay." He kept his tone soothing. "He can't hurt you now. You've got friends here, people who will do everything they can to protect you." He was one of them. And at the moment, he would love to get his hands on this Edmund character.

"No." Meagan had stopped rocking, but shook her

head, the motion adamant. "You can't protect me. No one can. Edmund is slick. He's killed before. And he'll kill again."

"He's a killer?" What kind of man had she gotten tangled up with? A thug? A mob boss?

"I don't have proof. At least not evidence that will stand up in court. And definitely not with his team of fancy lawyers. But I have this."

She stood and moved to the desk in the corner of the room. After pulling open one of the drawers, she removed a thick book. Inside was a sheet of paper folded in thirds. She handed it to him, and he opened it. There was no signature. The salutation simply said "Edmund." A chill settled over him as he read.

I found her. But no one needs to know. Meet me in the atrium at midnight with $1,000,000 in unmarked bills, and I'll quietly disappear.

Hunter handed the letter back to her. "Found who?"

"I don't know. But I can make a good guess. I did some research, and four years before Edmund met me, he was engaged. Finding information on her was easy. Patti Wallace. She was the daughter of one of the prominent families in the area and regularly made it into the society pages of the local papers."

Meagan drew in a deep breath. "But the articles got more and more disconcerting. She had a lot of suspicious injuries. Lots of bruises, a dislocated shoulder and a broken arm, with an excuse to go along with each one. Then she disappeared."

"Disappeared?"

"Yep. They never found a body, and although they

questioned Edmund extensively, they were never able to prove anything."

"So you think Edmund killed his ex-fiancée, and someone found out about it and was blackmailing him?"

"That's exactly what I think. That someone was Edmund's gardener, Charlie."

"Did Charlie succeed?"

"Charlie's dead."

At his raised brows she continued, "There's an atrium in Edmund's house. That's where I found Charlie, his head bashed in with a brass candlestick. My fingerprints were all over it, because it was mine. Edmund had given it to me as a peace offering the first time he hit me. I hated it because of what it represented. But Edmund could never know. So I put it where he suggested, in my studio, and just kept my back to it while I painted."

Hunter's chest clenched. The fact that she could still paint, still create things of beauty under those circumstances, showed what she was made of.

"Anyway," she went on, "at the time of Charlie's death, Edmund had a solid alibi. He had supposedly gone to his house in Maine. The caretaker of the place vouched for him. So did the airline. *I* even backed up the story. That was where he said he was going, and I had no reason to question it."

Hunter remained silent and let her talk. Now that the barriers had come down, she was spilling everything.

"A month later, I found the blackmail letter. It was in the atrium, slipped between a boulder and the greenery behind it. I used to do a lot of my sketching in there, and one of my favorite places to sit was on that boulder overlooking the waterfall and pond. I believe that what I found was a copy of the one given to Edmund, that Charlie put it there for me, in case something went wrong."

"It was nice of him to warn you, but he should have taken what he found to the police. Then you could have gotten your life back. Instead he got greedy and left you to fend for yourself."

She shrugged, apparently not feeling any of the dislike for the man that he felt. "I considered Charlie a friend. But he had a gambling problem. A few days before he died, he told me he had borrowed money from some really bad dudes. I think they were going to kill him if he didn't pay up. So he was desperate. He saw this as his only way out."

Hunter frowned. He wasn't as quick to forgive as Meagan was. But something told him she wasn't one to hold grudges. Or judge people harshly. Maybe he could learn a thing or two from her.

She returned to the couch and sank down next to him. "The blow was delivered by someone left-handed. I am, so that made me a suspect. Especially when combined with the fact that I was in the house and my fingerprints were on the candlestick. But Edmund is left-handed, too. Knowing what I know now, I believe someone who looked like Edmund boarded that plane to Maine."

"Did you go to the police with any of this?"

"No. Without a body, I didn't have solid enough proof. Anybody could have written that blackmail letter. With Edmund's resources, he would have hired the best attorneys money could buy and gotten out of it. Then he would have killed me."

"So you faked your death."

She nodded. "If I'd just run away, he would have gone after my mom and sister. He had to believe I was dead." Her shoulders slouched and she looked over at him, her eyes sad. "And now I suppose you're going to turn me in."

Silence stretched between them for several moments while her comment circled through his mind. Telling the authorities in California was out of the question. No way was he going to take a chance on Edmund getting his hands on Meagan. Besides, she had no warrants out there. She had no warrants anywhere. They had run her prints through IAFIS, and, other than the murder charge, which had been dropped, she was clean.

Of course, there was the issue of the I-9. But he wasn't willing to turn her in for that, either.

"No, I'm not. But you have to guarantee me that you've come clean and told me everything."

She drew in a slow breath. "I have."

"I want to do some checking. I'd love to see this guy put away for a long time."

She straightened, her back ramrod straight. "No, he can't know. He can't even suspect that I'm alive."

He placed his hand over hers. "Meagan, can you trust me?"

Her eyes locked on to his and held. She seemed to be searching, but for what, he didn't know. Apparently she found it. The tension left her body, and she leaned back into the couch cushions.

"I trust you."

He gave her hand a squeeze. "There's one more thing. I need your promise that you won't run, no matter what happens."

As long as she stayed, he and the other Cedar Key officers had a chance of keeping her safe. She was no match for Edmund's power and brutality. Whatever happened, he had to keep her on Cedar Key.

Because now that he knew her story, he was more determined than ever to protect her.

FOUR

Everything on Meagan Berry's front porch was white— white siding, white front door, white railing and white deck boards. Even the Adirondack chair and matching side table were painted white.

But when Hunter eased to a stop in the driveway, a new object had been added. A shiny blue tin sat atop the small table, a spot of bright color in the midst of none.

He nodded in that direction. "Is that yours?"

Meagan followed his gaze. "It wasn't there when Darci picked me up this morning. But if I had to guess, I'd say Mrs. Tackett has been busy in the kitchen again. She's always baking or cooking something and sharing it."

He followed Meagan onto the porch and watched her remove the card taped to the lid.

"Just what I thought." She angled the note toward him. "*Thanks for being so sweet. I hope you like no-bake brownies.* And she signed it *Margaret Tackett.*" Meagan picked up the tin and unlocked the front door.

He frowned. More than a week had passed since the attempt on her life. But that didn't mean the person had given up. Maybe he was just waiting for her to let down her guard. "Has Mrs. Tackett ever made brownies for you before?"

"Brownies, cookies, cake, homemade vegetable soup, you name it." Meagan gave him a teasing smile. "Somehow, I don't think she's much of a threat."

He followed her inside, where she placed the tin on the counter and removed the lid. "Mmm, they look good."

He leaned forward and took a long sniff. Peanut butter, cocoa, nuts and…something else he couldn't quite place.

Meagan started to reach for one, but he held up a hand. "Wait. I'd feel better if we talked to Mrs. Tackett first."

"What, are you going to ask her if she poisoned my brownies?"

"No, I'm going to ask her if she *left* the brownies."

Meagan's eyes widened. "You think they might have come from someone else?"

"Probably not. But there's already been one attempt on your life. I'm not willing to risk the possibility that someone slipped poison into these and put your neighbor's name on the card. If Mrs. Tackett says she made them, fine. I'll even have one with you."

Meagan pressed the lid back on. "All right. Let's go visit my neighbor."

When Mrs. Tackett answered their knock, an enticing aroma wafted out the door. Hunter's stomach rumbled in response. The next item on his agenda would be dinner. Nothing nearly as enticing as whatever Mrs. Tackett had made. More like leftovers. Unless he wanted to go out. Maybe he could convince Meagan to go with him.

She stepped forward to greet the older woman, then got right to the point. "This is going to sound strange, but did you leave a tin of no-bake brownies on my porch today?"

Mrs. Tackett's brows lifted, deepening the lines running across her forehead. "No, they weren't from me. Did you check with Sydney Tanner? She likes to bake."

"No, I—I haven't." Meagan's voice was weak and held a slight quiver. "Maybe I'll do that."

She made her way toward the sidewalk. Her eyes were round, and her face had lost three shades of color.

He touched a hand to the small of her back. "Are you okay?"

"The brownies came from whoever is trying to kill me. If you hadn't been with me…" She let the thought trail off, apparently unwilling to voice the likely outcome. He didn't want to think about it, either.

"We need to call the police."

She gave him a weak smile. "You *are* the police."

"We need a policeman who's on duty. They'll take the tin and turn it over to Levy County. Then it'll go to a lab for the contents to be tested. I'm guessing they'll find an ingredient the recipe doesn't call for." One intended to kill her.

His chest tightened. She was right. If he hadn't been there, she wouldn't have given it a second thought. She would have eaten one of the brownies immediately. Maybe two or three.

He called 911, then pocketed his phone. "How about letting me take you to dinner once the police report is done?"

She stepped onto her porch and unlocked the front door. "I don't think I can eat. For some reason, I've lost my appetite."

That sense of protectiveness that had filled him earlier surged up again, stronger than ever. "I don't want to leave you alone."

"You'll have to at some point."

"Not if I can help it." He followed her inside. "Any chance Edmund is behind all this?"

She looked at him askance. "Making poisoned no-bake brownies? No way."

"Based on everything you've told me, I would tend to agree. So what else can you tell me about him, besides that he's big and tough?"

"That's not Edmund."

"What?"

She sat on the couch, and Hunter settled in next to her.

"Edmund is tall and slender. Very cultured. But as cold as ice."

"So who is the big, tough guy who's been looking for you?"

"Lou. He works for Edmund. Lou will keep looking till he finds me. Then he'll give Edmund my whereabouts, and Edmund will come after me himself. He wouldn't give that pleasure up to anyone."

That made sense. But there was still one piece Hunter hadn't been able to fit into the puzzle. Before he could voice the question, the doorbell rang. It was Gary, another of his colleagues.

Once Gary had finished his investigation and left with the suspicious blue tin, Hunter turned to Meagan. "I never got a definitive answer on dinner."

"That's because I'm undecided."

"Come on, it beats sitting here alone. As long as you're with me, you'll have your own personal body-guard."

The corners of her mouth quirked up. "You can't imagine how appealing that is."

"I know *I'd* rest easier."

He followed her out the door, then helped her into his truck. After starting the engine, he let it idle. "There's one thing I don't understand. Supposedly the attempts on your life are in retaliation for you killing someone."

"I've been trying to figure that out myself. I can't see those accusations coming from Edmund. He never once insinuated that I had anything to do with Charlie's murder."

Hunter shifted into reverse and backed into the street. "What about Charlie's family? Maybe a girlfriend or wife?"

"Charlie wasn't married. I don't think he had a girlfriend, either."

"How well did you know him?"

"Pretty well. He lived in a cottage on Edmund's property. He wasn't highly educated, but he had a tender side and loved poetry." She released a wistful sigh. "We used to trade books back and forth. He had one that we both loved—an old volume of classic poetry. A few hours after I discovered his body, I found it in the atrium, about twenty feet from where he was killed. I think he was leaving it for me."

Hunter eased to a stop, then made a right on D Street. He would head toward Dock, where several restaurants overlooked the water.

"Did anyone question the fact that Charlie had been killed inside the house late at night, when he had his own place on the property?"

"Not really. Charlie was responsible for maintaining all the plants in the atrium. So he was in and out all the time, had a key and everything. It was a little odd, though, for him to have come in late at night, after I had gone to bed. At the time, I just figured he'd forgotten something. So I didn't really question it. When he turned up dead, I thought he couldn't pay his debt in cash, so they'd made him pay with his life. Then I found the blackmail note."

"So Charlie was desperate for money and figured he'd get it the easy way. He tried blackmailing Edmund and it backfired."

She nodded. "He should have known better than to—"

Just ahead of them a beat-up red Camaro flew right though the stop sign at Third. Hunter jammed on the brakes and jerked the wheel to the left, barely missing the rear bumper of the old sports car. A familiar figure sat at the wheel. No, he couldn't let this go. The kid was going to kill someone.

"I know I'm not on duty, but I've got to go after him before someone gets hurt."

Meagan's eyes were wide. The close call had shaken her as badly as it had him. "Do you know him?"

He did a one-eighty and took off after the Camaro. "Donny Blanchard. He used to be one of the kids in my Sunday school class. About three years ago he dropped out of church and has been getting into trouble ever since. Nothing serious. Just mischief."

Hunter followed the car through several turns until it made a left onto Airport Road. Since it led nowhere but the airport, they were the only two vehicles on the road. Which gave him the perfect conditions for what he needed to do.

He accelerated to ease up next to the other car and was met with Donny's grinning face. The kid wasn't speeding. If he hadn't just run a stop sign, Hunter wouldn't even have gone after him.

When Donny showed no signs of stopping, Hunter

pointed to the side of the road. When that didn't work, he crept closer, until Meagan could have reached over and wrapped her fingers around the kid's throat. Except she was too busy maintaining a death grip on the door handle.

Finally, Donny jammed on the brakes and pulled over. Hunter stopped in front of him and walked back to the car. Donny stared through the driver's side window, still holding on to that cocky grin.

Hunter knocked twice. "Roll down the window."

Finally, Donny complied, but the cockiness remained. "You can't give me a ticket. You're not on duty."

The words almost didn't register. The odor did. Alcohol. Heavy. The kid was drinking and driving.

Hunter swallowed hard. Fire started deep in his gut, searing a path upward and exploding through his mind. He grabbed the kid by the shirt collar and jerked him toward the window.

"Hey, man, let go of me."

The cockiness so obvious moments earlier had fled without a trace. But Hunter wasn't finished yet. Not by a long shot. Red-hot fury pumped through his veins. The kid was drunk. At age eighteen, that in itself was illegal. But he had also just endangered the lives of everyone in Cedar Key.

Hunter gave him a firm shake. "You're driving drunk." His voice was several decibels louder than normal. "You could have killed someone."

"I'm not drunk." Fear had replaced the cockiness in his eyes. "I had a few beers. That's all. No hard stuff."

"You're impaired. You ran a stop sign and almost hit us. There could have been someone walking, crossing the road. Or someone in a small car." A Honda Civic.

Broad-sided. Pushed sideways thirty feet from the force of the impact and pinned against a tree.

He tried to erase the image from his mind, but it wouldn't leave, wouldn't even fade. Every detail was as crisp and clear as it had been four years ago. The fury pounded harder.

He gave the kid another yank. His head was now halfway through the window opening. Hunter would have punched him if he could get away with it. "You shouldn't drink. Period." He shouted the words, even though the kid's face was inches from his own. "But if you do, don't *ever* be stupid enough to get behind the wheel of a car. Do you hear me?"

Donny didn't answer, just stared with wide, fear-filled eyes.

Hunter gave him another shake. "Do you hear me?"

"Y-yes, sir."

"Don't *ever* do that again."

"N-no, sir. I won't. Ever. I promise."

Hunter released his grip on the kid's collar one finger at a time as the tidal wave subsided. He needed to call 911, get Gary back out. Someone had to get Donny off the street before he killed someone.

When Hunter glanced back at his truck, Meagan was watching him through the rear window. As soon as his eyes met hers, she turned away. Uneasiness darkened the edges of his mind.

A few minutes later, he left Donny in Gary's capable hands and walked back to the truck. After sliding into the driver's seat, he glanced over at Meagan. The same fear he had seen on Donny's face was reflected in her eyes. The uneasiness intensified.

"He was drinking and driving. He could have killed

someone. I'm just trying to keep him from ruining his life."

She nodded, but didn't speak. A wall had gone up, and she was retreating behind it.

He had to make her understand. "Kids like that don't respond to namby-pamby pleas to do the right thing. You've got to be tough on them."

She nodded again and swallowed hard. "I think I'd rather go home. I'm really not hungry."

His heart sank. Everything between them had changed. She was now afraid of him. Or at the least, guarded around him. Given her past, he could understand why. He had to make her see that he wasn't like Edmund. Or any other abusive man she had known.

"Donny used to be a good kid. I'm worried about him. I'm trying to get him back on the right track."

"It's okay." She tried to force a smile. At least that was what he thought it was. One side of her mouth quivered but didn't manage to really lift. She gave up on the attempt. "I just want to go home. It's been a long day."

He heaved a sigh. "All right. I'll take you home." He had no choice. He would make sure the house was secure and pray like crazy that she would be safe till morning.

As he began moving back down Airport Road, regret bore down on him, guilt over the way he had handled the situation with Donny. Yes, kids like that needed firmness. Someone who cared enough to come down hard on them when necessary. Tough love. But that wasn't what he had given.

Because standing next to the runway back there, he hadn't been looking at an eighteen-year-old kid. He'd been seeing a forty-year-old man arguing with cops, obstinate and without remorse, while rescue workers struggled to free a young woman who lay pinned and dying in a mass of mangled metal.

No matter how much time passed, he would never erase the image. Or stem the anger that surged through him every time he remembered.

He wanted Meagan to trust him, not fear him. And he had made progress. But tonight, he had blown it. He had lost control.

And Meagan had watched.

A bell jangled, and Meagan turned from stocking a shelf in time to see two familiar figures enter the store. Darci's mother was an older version of Darci, with the same deep brown hair and vibrant blue eyes. She currently held the hand of her grandson, Jayden.

Darci hurried around the counter and swept the towheaded child into her arms. "Hi, sweetie. How's my boy? Did you miss Mommy?"

Instead of responding, Jayden's attention remained on the object he held, a toy cell phone. Now that both hands were free, his thumbs worked over the screen, creating a series of beeps.

He stiffened his body, a cue that he wanted down, and she placed him on the floor.

"Let me grab my purse, and I'll be ready." For once, Darci was subdued, lines of concern marring her features.

When she reached the door, her mom gave her a hug. "It's going to be okay. Whatever happens, God will give us the strength to handle it."

As Meagan watched them step outside, a wave of homesickness washed through her, an intense longing to see her own mother again. Three months had passed since she had last heard her voice, and much longer since she had talked freely. Throughout the year before she'd had to disappear, she'd been guarded, infusing her tone with false cheer, saying everything was fine when it wasn't. Otherwise, her mother would have charged right over, at the risk of all of their lives, demanding to know what Edmund was doing to make her girl unhappy. Her mom had always been her protector, champion and best friend.

But Meagan didn't begrudge Darci this time with her mom, especially this afternoon. Jayden was two and hadn't yet started to talk. Darci claimed she had talked late, too, and had been making up for it ever since. But coupling that with some other signs, she couldn't deny it any longer. Something was wrong.

So this afternoon, the three of them were headed to Gainesville to see a child psychologist. Hopefully, the diagnosis would be good—a little delayed development that would work itself out in time. Although no one had mentioned the word *autism*, Meagan had been thinking it and was pretty sure Darci was, too.

With a sigh, Meagan returned to arranging the figurines she had unboxed before Darci's mother came in. Just as she finished, the bell on the front door sounded. Tension spiked through her. She drew in a calming breath and tried to slow her racing pulse. She worked in a gift shop. She couldn't recoil in fear every time a customer walked in.

This time it wasn't a customer. It was Hunter, in uniform, with a gun at his hip. The sight was comforting. But he wasn't the only one looking out for her. A killer was loose on the island. And for whatever reason, she was the target. So Cedar Key had enlisted the aid of Levy County. A plainclothes detective was currently watching her house, with another keeping an eye on the store. A third was inside, inconspicuous but ever vigilant. Hunter was making regular stops, as were the other officers. Whoever was after her would be hard-pressed to get anywhere near her.

Unless it was Edmund.

She climbed onto the bar stool behind the counter and gave Hunter an uneasy smile.

He returned it, his no more comfortable than hers. Things had been strained between them since the incident with the kid in the Camaro. As she had gotten to know Hunter over the past month, he had impressed her more than she wanted to admit. He was kind, gentle, caring—a true public servant. Without even realizing it, she had begun to look on him as a hero, a knight in shining armor.

Two nights ago, that image had been shattered. He was just a man, the same as the others she had known. Sweet and charming, but capable of abuse if provoked. She had wanted to believe he was somehow different, which had been stupid. She didn't believe in fairy tales, hadn't even as a kid. Why start now?

Hunter rested a forearm against the counter. "Everything okay?"

"Everything's fine. Darci left a few minutes ago."

"So you're by yourself."

"As by myself as I can be with half of Cedar Key and Levy County watching me." And others in an unofficial capacity, like Hunter's friend Blake.

"Right now, all those extra eyes are good." There was a seriousness in his tone that was reflected in his gaze.

"Believe me, I'm not complaining."

She reached for a spiral notebook she had placed on the counter earlier. When she met Hunter's eyes again, the seriousness was still there. He had something else to say.

"The lab results came back on the brownies."

"And?"

"Cyanide."

She swallowed hard. She had expected the tests to show some kind of poison, but hearing it confirmed filled her gut with lead.

"Is that even available?"

"Not for the average person. Not in the US, anyway."

She shook her head. "I came so close to eating them. I would have if you hadn't stopped me." Her gaze locked with his, and the last of the stiffness between them dissolved. "You saved my life."

He lifted his hand, then, halfway to her face, let it fall. "It's all in a day's work." His mouth curled up, the smile at odds with the seriousness still lingering in his eyes.

And it was that seriousness, and the sincerity behind it, that was wreaking havoc with her defenses. She flipped open the notebook, thankful for a ready distraction. Here she was, three months out of a yearlong nightmare, and ready to head down the same dangerous path. She straightened her spine, determined to hold on to her resolve. Hopefully, her brain had the sense to never again let her fall for another man's charm, even if her heart didn't.

She dropped her eyes to the page. "I figured while Darci was gone, I'd do some creative work. I'm designing brochures for the store. I thought if we put them in some of the other establishments around town, it might help to drum up business."

Hunter nodded. "Good idea. You know, Darci's glad she hired you."

"I hope so." Because most of the time Meagan felt as if she really wasn't needed.

But not according to her boss. Even though she had never hired staff in the past, Darci claimed she wanted a part-time assistant so she could spend more time with Jayden.

Meagan knew better. It was an excuse, a way to offer much-needed help without making her feel like a charity case. If anyone deserved a break, it was Darci. She spent her whole life doing for others. If the God she served was as loving as she claimed, He'd fix this problem with Jayden.

Hunter tapped the counter. "I guess I'll leave you to it. I'll be back at six to take you home."

Meagan watched him walk out the front and get into his patrol car. For several moments after he drove away, she stared at the vacated parking space. If she had to have a cop in her business, why did it have to be someone like Hunter, whose sweetness and charm and good looks sent a constant barrage of cannonballs flying at her defenses? Why couldn't it be someone old and married?

She propped her elbows on the counter and rested her chin in her hands. The noonday sun streamed in the front door and plate-glass window, falling across the painting she had displayed there. Completed last weekend, it rested on an easel next to the door, a pelican on a dock set against a blazing sunset, palm fronds hanging in the foreground. Like all her paintings now, it was signed M. Berry.

Her artwork provided a nice secondary income, helping supplement her part-time job at Darci's. Or maybe her job at Darci's supplemented her painting. Either way, she needed both to survive.

Throughout the afternoon, only a handful of customers came into the store, giving her large blocks of time to work on the brochure. As promised, Hunter arrived a few minutes before six to take her home. While she closed up and bade the detective farewell, Hunter waited at the door. No longer on duty, he was dressed in jeans and a button-up shirt. The bottom tip of a holster peeked out from below the hem.

Moments later he slid into the truck across from her. "Have you talked to Darci yet?"

"Not yet." Meagan entwined her fingers in her lap and fought against the urge to squirm. "I will, though. I just haven't found a good time."

"We talked about this a week ago." He pulled away from the curb and began moving down Second Street. "Darci needs to know, but I think you should be the one to tell her."

"I know. And I will." Sometime. Once she got up the courage. She was just putting it off, hanging on to her job as long as possible. Because once Darci knew she had lied to her, she would likely lose that job.

Hunter slowed to make the left onto Fifth Street and glanced over at her. "Do you trust her?"

"Yes, I trust her. But that's not the point. I lied to her. She would have every reason to fire me."

"I know Darci really well. And I think I'm pretty safe in assuming that she'll stick by you. But she needs to know." He eased to a stop in the driveway and turned off the ignition. "If you don't tell her, I will."

Meagan crossed her arms and glared at him. "I said I'll tell her. You don't have to threaten me."

Without waiting for a response, she stepped from the truck and slammed the door. Wearing a badge didn't give Hunter the right to order her around. Of course, he probably claimed that right because of his status as a man.

Like every man she had ever known. At least those she'd been closest to. First came the charm. Then the control. Then the rage when other people, and life in general, didn't fall into place. It was one of the first things she had learned as a child, almost before learning to walk, a lesson that was pounded into her anew each time her dad had left her mother bruised and bloody.

Meagan strode toward the house and climbed the porch steps. The detective was somewhere nearby, watching them. But he was easy to ignore. Right now, she just wanted to get away from Hunter's prying gaze, into the privacy of her home.

She pulled the key from her purse. Hunter was beside her before she could unlock the door.

"Look, Meagan, I'm not trying to threaten you."

"Do this or else—that's a threat, any way you look at it." She jammed the key into the lock.

"I didn't mean it as a threat. I'm just giving you a nudge."

Yeah, a nudge. A sharp jab with a cattle prod to produce the desired result. She had lots of experience with nudges. They could be quite painful.

She turned to face Hunter. She had seen him lose it. He had dragged the kid halfway through the window before he got control of himself. Was he capable of the same brutality as her father and Edmund? Maybe, maybe not. She wasn't going to get close enough to find out.

She heaved a sigh. "I'll talk to Darci when she comes in tomorrow."

As she turned toward the door, a series of sounds stopped her cold—an almost imperceptible whoosh, following by a *thwing* and a grunt, all in a fraction of a second. She spun around. Hunter stood clutching his upper arm as blood oozed between his fingers. Next to him, an arrow was frozen in space, its tip buried in the wood siding.

Her mind shut down. Hunter was saying something, but she couldn't make sense of the words. Somewhere deep in her subconscious, she knew she needed to move. But she was rooted to the spot.

Hunter reached around her to open the door, then pushed her inside. He stumbled in after her and closed and locked the door.

"Meagan. Don't lose it on me, baby." He grasped her shoulder with his free hand and gave her a little shake. He was still using the other to staunch the flow of blood.

"Edmund." It was the only word that would form.

Hunter released her to reach for his cell phone. "Edmund? You think Edmund did this?"

She nodded. Her brain was slowly kicking back into gear. "Edmund's biggest hobby is archery."

Sirens screamed in the distance, pulling her the rest of the way back. Hunter was trying to hold the phone in his free hand and dial with his thumb, but his fingers didn't seem to be working right. Her gaze shifted to his shoulder. Blood had soaked through the sleeve and traced multiple paths down his arm. And she had stood there like an imbecile.

She took the phone from him. Maybe the sirens were for them, but maybe they weren't. "Let me."

After placing the 911 call, she led him to the kitchen and eased him into a chair. The color had leached from his face, and beads of sweat dotted his brow.

"How bad do you think it is?"

He shifted his position and grimaced. "Not as bad as it could have been. But judging from the amount of blood, I'm afraid it tore through a good bit of muscle."

The sirens drew closer. The detective watching the

house had apparently called for backup. The fire guys should be right on their tail.

"You stay seated."

She left Hunter to jog to the door. Two law enforcement vehicles came to a stop at the curb, one Cedar Key Police, the other Levy County Sheriff. Another sheriff vehicle was stopped down the street. Maybe Edmund was inside. Not likely. He was too cunning to get caught.

The Cedar Key Fire rescue truck stopped behind the other vehicles, and Wade and Joe jumped out. She waved them inside. "Hunter was hit. He's in the kitchen."

Two law enforcement officers met her on the porch— Gary and Deputy Baker, according to his nameplate. Baker proceeded to examine the arrow, and Gary followed her inside, where she offered him a seat on the couch. She took the recliner. The activity was helping her keep the panic at bay. She would give her statement while Wade and Joe temporarily patched up Hunter and got him ready to transport. She could fall apart later, once everyone was gone and Hunter was on his way to the hospital.

Gary pulled a small notebook from his pocket. "What happened?"

"I don't know. Hunter was leaving, and I had turned to go inside. So I didn't see anything."

Gary asked several more questions that she couldn't answer. If she had had the presence of mind to look across the street when it happened, she might have seen someone run away. Maybe Hunter had.

Static sounded from Gary's radio, followed by a male voice. Her heart fell. The suspect was still at large. But they had found the weapon, a Parker crossbow. The suspect had dropped it in the bushes two doors down.

As Wade and Joe carried Hunter out on a stretcher,

Meagan's heart twisted. He was on his way to the hospital because of her. He could have been killed.

Or she could have been with Darci when Edmund attacked. And Darci could have been killed, leaving her precious little boy without a mother *or* father.

Meagan had promised Hunter that she wouldn't run, no matter what happened. That was a promise she was going to have to break. Staying would endanger the lives of everyone she cared about.

So tomorrow morning, she would go see Darci. After all Darci had done for her, Meagan couldn't leave without saying goodbye. Then she would cash last week's paycheck and put it with the eight hundred dollars she had saved from selling her paintings. Finally, she would take a cab to the Greyhound station in Chiefland, thirty minutes away. From there, she would decide where to go. As far from Cedar Key as she could afford.

Maybe somewhere large this time, a big city where she could get lost in the throngs of people. Three months ago, Cedar Key had seemed like the perfect choice. She had wanted somewhere far from California, preferably warm and small enough to get around without a car. Though she had never been to Cedar Key before, a childhood friend used to vacation there, and listening to her stories, the place had seemed magical. Of course, at twelve years old, everything had seemed magical. By twenty-four, the knocks of life had pretty well destroyed the magic of childhood.

Now she wasn't going for magical. Or even warm. As far as getting around without a car, large cities had mass transit.

She would be starting over in a big metropolis with less than half the cash she'd had when she came to Cedar

Key. The thought made her blood run cold. But there was one thought that scared her more.

Edmund had found her.

Tonight she would be safe. All night long, cops would be watching her house. Then tomorrow, she would run.

As she made her plans, something kept niggling at the back of her mind, the sense that something was off. She walked into the kitchen and opened the fridge. She wasn't hungry, but anything she didn't eat tonight would go to waste. The unopened things she would give to Darci.

Meagan popped a bowl of leftover spaghetti into the microwave, then stood watching it turn. Suddenly it hit her. Her mind had immediately gone to Edmund because of his love of archery. There was only one problem.

Edmund wouldn't have missed.

But maybe he hadn't been aiming for her. Maybe his target had been Hunter. Especially if he thought there was anything between the two of them.

She dismissed that thought also. If Edmund had wanted to hit Hunter, the shot wouldn't have been to his shoulder.

It would have been straight through his heart.

FIVE

A familiar tune sounded in the distance. But Hunter didn't want to listen to music. Actually, he didn't want to hear anything. The silent darkness that enveloped him was soothing.

Except for the pain, an annoying throb in his shoulder. If he could just sink further into the darkness...

He reached for the spare pillow to throw it over his face. Searing pain shot through his left shoulder, bringing him fully awake. Memories of the prior night rushed back to him. Bringing Meagan home. Getting shot. With an arrow, of all things. It had grazed his left arm, its metal tip slicing a jagged path across his deltoid, laying the flesh wide open.

He swiped his right hand down his face, trying to brush the sleep from his eyes. It had been a rough night. He had tried to remain on his back, but he was a side sleeper, alternating between his left and right throughout the night. More times than he could count, he had stopped midroll as pain jarred him awake.

The music sounded again. Now fully conscious, he recognized it instantly. Who was calling at that early hour? He turned on his good side and reached for the phone, his eyes falling on the window as he did. Light filtered in between the slats in the miniblinds. *Bright* light. Maybe it wasn't so early, after all.

He mumbled a tired "hello" into the phone.

Darci's cheery voice greeted him.

"What time is it?" He squinted at the alarm clock next to his bed. Nine-fourteen. That couldn't be right.

"It's a quarter after nine. Are you all right? Meagan told me what happened."

"Yeah, I'm okay. They cleaned everything up and sewed me back together. But I'm going to be in a sling for a while."

"Meagan's leaving."

"What?" If there was any grogginess still lingering in his brain, it was gone now. "What do you mean, she's leaving?"

"She stopped by the store to tell me goodbye."

An odd sadness pricked his heart. She hadn't bothered to tell *him* goodbye.

But why should she? They didn't have any kind of special relationship. Not even a real friendship. All his dealings with her were as a cop protecting a citizen. Nothing more than that. On either side.

Besides, she had a good reason for avoiding him. She had made him a promise. And now she was breaking it.

"Where is she going?"

"I don't know. Actually, *she* doesn't know. She was headed to the bus station in Chiefland and is going to pick a place and buy a ticket when she gets there."

"How is she getting to Chiefland?"

"She called a cab."

He struggled to a sitting position. Meagan was on her way out of Cedar Key, out of their lives. Relationship or not, he wasn't ready to let her go.

She needed him. She needed all of them. She was lost

and alone. And Edmund was closing in. She didn't stand a chance if she left their protection. Edmund would get to her in no time.

If he hadn't already.

Hunter put Darci on speakerphone and laid down the phone to struggle into some shorts. "How long ago did she leave?"

"Maybe fifteen minutes. I tried calling you two other times."

Two times? He must have been dead to the world. It was probably the combination of the pain medication and the fact that he didn't get home until 3:00 a.m. And the six hours that he did spend in bed, he was either in a tense state of alertness, consciously trying to stay on his back, or falling into a deep enough sleep to roll onto his left side, which had jarred him awake.

He pulled out a T-shirt, then put it back in the drawer in favor of something he could don without lifting his left arm, another button-up shirt.

"Are you still there?" Darci's words cut into his thoughts, reminding him how long it had been since he had spoken.

"I'm here. But I'm going after her."

"I thought you might."

There was a smile in Darci's tone, almost an *I knew it* or an *I told you so.* He knew exactly what she was thinking. Darci was a hopeless romantic. At least where everyone else was concerned. She herself avoided relationships like the plague. In that way, she was a bit of a hypocrite.

Well, she could cling to whatever fantasies she wanted to have. Regardless of the attraction that sparked between him and Meagan, he wasn't in the market for love. And neither was Meagan. She had too many issues. In

fact, she had *complicated* written all over her. And he
didn't do complicated.

He ended the call and pulled out a pair of shoes that
didn't involve laces. When he had finished wrestling
with the last of his shirt buttons, he resecured the sling
and dashed out the door. His friend Blake had ventured
out in the middle of the night to bring him home. But
this trip he would make by himself.

As he left Cedar Key and headed up the highway,
he kept his eyes peeled for a cab. He probably wouldn't
overtake her on 24. She'd had too much of a head start.
Maybe 345.

He didn't overtake her there, either. But as he drove
into the Greyhound bus station, a taxi was pulling out.
He chose a parking space near the door and hurried inside. Meagan stood at the ticket counter, counting out
bills. He charged up beside her and held up a hand. "Stop
the sale."

The customer service representative raised her brows
and looked to Meagan for instruction.

Meagan spun toward him, eyes flashing. "You don't
control my life." She shifted her gaze back to the Greyhound employee. "Continue, please. I'm buying the
ticket."

Hunter mentally took a step back. He would have to
treat her gently. At his initial show of force, her defenses
had gone up and her claws had come out. She had a defi-
nite stubborn streak. "Meagan, wait."

"Don't try to talk me out of it. My mind is made up."

"Come on, Meagan. I don't want you to be alone." He
heaved a sigh. "Let me take you home. At least come
outside with me where we can talk."

Indecision flashed across her features, and her hand
tightened around the stack of bills still on the counter.

He sought the words to convince her to stay, without broadcasting her situation to everyone in the station. But before he could voice them, the Greyhound rep reached across the counter and patted her hand.

"Go on, sweetie, try to fix things with your man. If it doesn't work out, you can come back. We'll be here."

Color crept up Meagan's cheeks. "He's not my—"

The rep continued as if she hadn't spoken. "In the meantime, I don't think you'll have any problem holding your own." Her eyes went to his sling, and a knowing smile curved her lips. "It looks like he got the short end of the stick on this one."

Meagan's face registered confusion. Then understanding dawned, and her eyes widened. "No, that's not— I mean, I didn't— That was—"

Hunter put his arm around her shoulders and led her away from the counter.

Once outside, she turned to face him. "She thought you and I were…" Her words trailed off.

"A couple." He finished the thought for her. "And that we had a lover's spat, and you beat me up."

"That's ridiculous." The corners of her mouth quivered, as if she was trying to stifle a smile. It broke through, anyway, followed by a nervous giggle, then full-blown laughter.

He started laughing, too, just because she was, and because seeing her laugh brought him unexpected joy.

She put a hand over her mouth and snorted, which was somehow cute instead of unsophisticated. It only made her laugh harder. And he recognized the laughter for what it was—a much-needed release of months of pent-up emotion. All the hurt and fear and anger came rushing out, purged through the healing act of laughter.

Finally, it subsided, and she wiped tears from her

face. "That felt good. That's the first time I've laughed in months."

"Laughter does good, like a medicine."

She smiled up at him. "Is that a wise old proverb?"

"Yeah, it's in the Bible. Actually it says 'a merry heart,' but same difference."

"I can see that."

"There's a lot of wisdom in the Good Book."

"So I've heard." She looked down and shifted her weight from one foot to the other. When she once again met his gaze, her eyes held sadness. "I can't go back with you."

His heart fell. "If you leave, he'll still find you. From what you've told me, he doesn't seem like the type to give up."

Hunter had checked out her story, and everything she had said was true. There was just one thing she hadn't told him—that she looked so much like Edmund's ex-fiancée it was eerie.

"This wasn't Edmund. Edmund is still a very real threat, always will be. But if Edmund had shot that arrow, he wouldn't have missed. There are at least two people who want me dead. And I'm not putting anyone else in danger. You could have been killed last night."

"But I wasn't. All I got was a flesh wound."

She frowned. "You can't tell me that. I was there. I saw the blood."

"Okay, it was a little deeper than a flesh wound. But it'll heal."

"As long as I stay, no one is safe. Not you, not Darci, and not anyone else I get close to. Whether it's Edmund or someone else who has targeted me, it's my problem. If anything happened to any of you guys, I'd never forgive myself."

And he would never forgive *himself* if she became a statistic—another sad story of a life snuffed out by a jealous ex-boyfriend. His chest tightened.

"Your staying in Cedar Key is the only chance we have of catching whoever is doing this. If you leave, you'll spend the rest of your life looking over your shoulder, living in fear. Stay here, and you'll eventually be free. Freedom, Meagan. Think of what that would feel like."

She drew in a shaky breath and closed her eyes. But not before he saw the battle going on there—the appeal of her own safety warring with the desire to protect her friends.

He forged ahead, seizing the opportunity while she was wavering. "Give us a chance. It's only been a little over two weeks since the note was left at Darci's. Let me catch this guy." He rested his hands on her shoulders and gave them a squeeze. "I'm asking you to trust me."

She finally opened her eyes. "All right. But I want security stepped up while I'm at the store. I don't want anyone to be able to get near me as long as Darci is around."

"We can do that." Actually, he wanted security stepped up around her house, too. A few inches either direction last night and one or the other of them could have been dead.

He walked her to the truck, and as he got into the driver's seat, his gaze fell on the door of the station. The clerk at the counter was watching them through the glass.

He nodded toward the building. "I think she's happy we're working it out."

Meagan rolled her eyes.

He pulled out of the parking lot and headed toward the highway.

Meagan looked over at him. "By the way, I told Darci."

"Everything?"

"Everything."

"What did she say?"

"Well, she didn't say whether I still had my job, because at that time it was a moot point. I was leaving."

"I'm guessing you still have your job."

He turned onto Highway 345, and within moments was stuck behind a truck and flatbed trailer loaded with construction supplies. He slowed and waited for an opportunity to pass.

"I'm assuming they never found who shot me."

"Not that I heard. I think someone would have told me."

"I'll call the station when we get back, just to check."

Once traffic cleared, he stepped on the gas and eased into the other lane. As his front wheel passed the rear wheel of the trailer, a small bag fell in front of him. A fraction of a second later, there was a solid crunch under his right front tire.

Meagan frowned. "That didn't sound good."

"24 is just ahead. I'm going to make the turn, then pull over."

Two minutes later, he dropped his speed to a crawl, eased off the shoulder and killed the engine. As soon as he stepped out, a soft hiss reached him. *No, not a flat tire.* He would have to call for help. Changing a tire with one arm in a sling was beyond his capabilities.

He rounded the front bumper and found the source of the hiss. Three screw heads rested snugly against the rubber treads, their shafts buried in the tire. There were likely more.

Meagan opened the door. "Is the tire okay?"

"Depends on your definition of *okay*. I found out what I hit. A bag of screws. I'm losing air fast."

"Do you have a spare?"

He shrugged, then winced. "I have one, but it's not going to do me a whole lot of good. Changing a tire with one arm in a sling isn't a skill I've mastered."

"I can do it."

He looked at her askance. "You?"

"Don't look so shocked. I've driven since I was sixteen. And with no man in the house, I learned pretty young how to do things for myself." She climbed out of the truck. "Where is your jack and spare tire?"

"The jack is behind the rear seat. The spare is back there." He pointed to the bed of the truck. But he would get them. No way was he going to let a woman change his tire while he stood idly by.

Once they had retrieved the items, she squatted down in front of the tire and set to work on the lug nuts, leveraging her body to break them loose. This was a side of Meagan he hadn't seen before, and it filled him with a new sense of respect. But he shouldn't be surprised. She had to be pretty self-sufficient to have done what she did to get away from Edmund. And lived to tell about it.

"What happened to your father?"

"When I was ten, he beat my mother so badly he almost killed her. It wasn't the first time, but it was the last."

Hunter shook his head. From an abusive father to Edmund. Had she had any examples of how a man was supposed to treat a woman?

She loosened the final nut and positioned the jack. "He got out of jail six years later and did everything he could to win her back. But after so long living without having to tiptoe around a man, constantly afraid of accidentally setting him off, Mom wasn't about to give up her freedom. All his apologies and promises didn't faze her. He finally gave up and moved away. I was sixteen then and haven't heard from him since."

Meagan shifted her position. The truck was jacked up far enough that the tire was no longer resting on the ground. She pulled it off, rolled it aside, then lifted the spare onto the lugs, helping to support it with one sneakered foot. A car sped toward them, coming from the direction of Cedar Key, and he glanced up as it passed.

His heart jumped to double time. It was a white sedan with tinted windows. He studied the car with keen alertness, trying to commit everything he could to memory over the next three or four seconds. There was a Cadillac emblem on the back. And a model he couldn't make out. Maybe a DeVille. Florida tag, number 56Y… He couldn't get the rest.

But that was at least something. Ever since Meagan was almost hit, everyone had been on the lookout for the white sedan. Apparently, it had been kept out of sight, maybe in a garage. Because no one had seen a car fitting that description. Until now.

Had the driver gotten wind of the fact that Meagan was leaving? Had he given up, figuring he had lost her? Or was he on his way to the bus station?

Hunter pulled out his cell phone. He would have the Chiefland police intercept him. And if that didn't work, he would run what information he had as soon as he got back to Cedar Key.

More than anything, he wanted to catch this guy. But this new development brought him a sliver of relief. Her stalker believed she had left Cedar Key. If she'd been sitting in his front seat, in full view behind the windshield, the guy would have known she was returning. Instead, she'd been crouched beside the truck. And he'd been standing at the front quarter panel, further blocking her from view. Yes, her stalker would believe she was gone.

And not coming back. Thanks to the flat tire.

All things work together for good...

Hunter smiled. Maybe what he had considered a major inconvenience had just bought Meagan a reprieve.

Meagan cruised down the main channel, her four-horse motor wide open. The sun on her face and the breeze in her hair did wonders for straightening out her tangled thoughts.

Yesterday, Darci had gotten the news they had all feared. After numerous tests, Jayden's psychologist had given a diagnosis—mild to moderate autism. Darci had accepted the news with quiet strength. But Meagan wasn't accepting anything. Fire pumped through her veins, anger that God would let this happen to someone so nice. Someone who didn't deserve it.

According to Darci, everyone had been praying—Darci, her mom, Hunter and most of their church. But God turned a deaf ear. If He didn't answer the prayers of good people like Darci, what chance did *she* have of ever being heard?

She eased to the edge of the channel to avoid the wake of an approaching powerboat. Finally being on the water again brought a wonderful sense of freedom. She'd been cooped up for so long, under the constant watchful eye of someone. Well, she still was; it just wasn't as obvious.

Today Hunter's friend Blake was the one hanging close, currently about thirty feet off her stern. She felt almost as safe with him as she did with Hunter. He was a former police detective, injured on the job. He walked with a limp and often used a cane, but he knew how to use a gun.

The one he carried was a pink Glock. He said it belonged to his wife. There was probably a story behind that, but Meagan didn't know him well enough to ask.

She eased back into the channel. A little farther and she would head southeast to Snake Key.

Almost two weeks had passed without incident. Apparently, whoever had been stalking her had finally given up. So yesterday she'd decided it was time to start living again. She hadn't bought a boat to leave it sitting idle in Darci's dad's backyard. And she wasn't living in a vacationer's paradise to restrict her comings and goings to work, home and the grocery store. Several of her paintings had sold. It was time to get busy and restock her inventory.

She had decided on Snake Key for several reasons. One, Blake said the fishing was good. He would be anchored just east of there, keeping her in his sight. Two, Snake Key was one of the islands that she hadn't yet visited. Three, it was much more open and a less popular destination than Seahorse Key or Atsena Otie, so she would have plenty of warning before anyone could get close enough to be a threat.

A wet, cold sensation against her feet drew her attention downward. About a quarter inch of water had pooled in the back of the boat. Worry chewed at the edges of her mind. It wasn't a lot, but it was too much to be sea spray. Besides, she was still in the channel.

She cast a glance over her shoulder. The Sea Ray was still back there. The sight helped to relieve the tension seeping into her shoulders. She wasn't alone. If anything went wrong, a simple hand motion would have Blake next to her in seconds.

Her gaze dipped again to her feet. The puddle was expanding. Now she had no doubt. Her boat was taking on water.

She looked around her, searching for the nearest island. None were close. Snake Key, Seahorse Key and Atsena Otie were equally distant. Her heart began to pound, and she reached for one of the life jackets. She could swim without one. She had proved it to herself over three months ago when she'd abandoned Edmund's boat in the middle of the lake and made a long, lone swim in the darkness. This would be nothing, especially with Blake to pluck her from the Gulf, if necessary.

As she dragged the life jacket onto her lap, dread trickled through her. One black strap dangled over her leg, its end cut. The plastic clasp was gone. She turned the life vest over and gasped. The orange nylon was shredded. Deep grooves marred the foam inside. She snatched the other jacket from its place on the floor. It, too, was destroyed.

Lead filled her gut, temporarily immobilizing her. What had happened to her boat wasn't wear and tear, failure due to age or accidental damage. It had been done intentionally. Someone had tampered with it so it would take on water, then ruined her life jackets, hoping she would drown. Her stalker hadn't given up.

And they were no closer to identifying him than when they had started. The information Hunter had on the sedan had led nowhere. There were three possible matches—a retired couple in Ocala, a single woman in Fanning Springs and a widow in The Villages. After questioning by law enforcement, all of them had been dismissed as possible suspects. Hunter had probably misread a number.

Meagan swung around to look at Blake, then gave him two sharp waves. In moments, he was beside her.

"I'm taking on water. I shouldn't have any problem getting to Snake Key, but hold on to my stuff, just in case." She handed him her phone, camera bag and sketch pad, then tossed the life jackets to him. They were worthless, but they were evidence.

She ignored his raised brows and gunned the motor. There would be time to explain later.

Halfway to Snake Key, her fear turned to desperation. She would never make it. Water was coming in more and more quickly, as if flowing through an ever expanding hole.

She threw a panicked glance at Blake, but he was already uncoiling a dock line. He tossed the end to her. "Tie this off to your boat."

She killed the motor, then made her way forward in a crouch, sloshing through six inches of water. The boat listed to one side, and her heart leaped into her throat. She crouched even lower, clutching the sides.

When she reached the front cleat, she made a knot with shaking fingers. Hopefully it would hold. If not, her boat would end up on the bottom of the Gulf.

She looked over at Blake. He was beside her, holding the two boats together. He extended his free hand. "Get on."

When she was aboard the Sea Ray, he gradually accelerated. But with every passing second, her hopes sank. They might save her boat, but the motor would be shot.

By the time they reached Snake Key, only the bow was visible above the waves, the motor submerged. Meagan jumped into the water, and moments later Blake was beside her, helping pull the waterlogged johnboat onto the shore. They tipped it on its side, and Blake bent to inspect it. Three nickel-sized holes penetrated the hull, hidden from above by the seat. He swept a finger across the edge of one, then rubbed his thumb and forefinger together.

"These were drilled, then filled with something that would dissolve after being in the water awhile." He reached for his phone. "We need to call the police. It looks like you're not out of danger, after all."

The police came in the form of Hunter Kingston. A fuming Hunter Kingston.

He stepped ashore and swooped down on her, eyes blazing. "What in the world were you thinking, coming out here alone?"

Blake crossed his arms over his chest. "Hey, what am I, chopped liver?"

Hunter glared at his friend, apparently not any happier with him than he was with her.

Blake glared right back. "Look, she caught me at the marina this morning and wanted to know if I was going out. I said I was, and she asked if she could tag along. She thought the danger was over. We all did. But she was still being cautious."

"You should have called me."

"Sorry, I didn't know you were her self-appointed guardian." Blake stepped closer and lowered his voice. "Or maybe there's more between you two than you're willing to admit."

In spite of the subdued tone, Meagan heard every word. Hunter didn't respond, just turned that angry glare on her. It wasn't nearly as intimidating with Blake there to absorb some of the hostility.

"You took chances today that were totally unnecessary." His voice was still raised.

"I didn't come out alone. I made sure someone was with me." Her volume matched his. She wasn't about to let him intimidate her. *He* was the one who was out of line. Police officers weren't supposed to yell at victims, even if they didn't agree with their choices.

She pointed a finger in his face. "You don't need to be treating me like an errant child. I didn't think I was taking chances. The sedan was gone. You saw it leave."

"Apparently it came back. Or the creep found another mode of transportation." Hunter's voice was still raised.

"Or maybe my boat was tampered with two or three weeks ago." It was possible. She hadn't been out since getting the threatening note.

Blake held up both palms. "I'm going to leave you two to iron this out on your own. I promised Allison fresh fish for dinner, and you're cutting into my fishing time." He dropped his hands and limped back to his boat.

When Hunter turned to face her again, some of the fire had left his eyes. "Please, just promise me you won't go out alone."

She heaved an exasperated sigh. It was as if he hadn't heard a word she had said. "I *didn't* go out alone. I was with Blake. He's law enforcement, just like you. He's trained, and he's got lots of experience. And just because there could still be some slim chance that I might be in danger, he went back and got Allison's gun. So I wasn't alone. Far from it." She planted her hands on her hips. "I don't think your concern is about me going out alone. I think it's about me going somewhere without telling you."

Hunter threw up his hands. "Okay. I admit it. I'm going crazy worrying about you. I have been ever since I read that note in Darci's store."

At his admission, her stomach rolled over and a watery weakness filled her legs. That didn't sound like simple professional concern.

She swallowed hard. "Do you worry about all your residents like that?"

He didn't answer immediately, just stared, searching her eyes. Or maybe he was searching within himself.

And suddenly, she didn't want to hear the answer. What if Blake was right? What if there really was more between them than Hunter was willing to admit?

What if there was more between them than *she* was willing to admit?

Please lie. Because I don't want to know the truth.

"No." His tone was soft, but heavy with resignation. "I don't worry about all my residents like that."

He began to walk back toward his boat.

"Hey, wait. Where are you going?"

He didn't respond.

She hurried after him. "I need to get my boat back home."

"We will."

"How?"

"Duct tape."

She waded into the water with him. Her camera bag and other items were on his seat. Thank goodness Blake had had the presence of mind to think about her things. When he left, she'd been too wrapped up in her argument with Hunter.

She cast him a doubt-filled glance. "You're really going to fix my boat with duct tape."

"Not fix it." He reached into a bin in the back and pulled out the roll of tape. "Just keep it afloat until we get back to Cedar Key."

He waded to shore with the tape in one hand and a towel draped over his shoulder. "First we'll move your motor to my back transom."

"Do you think it's salvageable?" She would keep the conversation on safe topics.

"I'm sure it'll need cleaning up, maybe the carburetor rebuilt." He moved away from the water's edge to lay the towel on dry ground, the tape on top. "I have a friend who's great with small-engine repair. He owes me a favor."

"But he doesn't owe *me* a favor."

"Don't worry about it. He's retired, so he's got lots of time on his hands. And he doesn't need the money. His tinkering is more of a hobby." Hunter smiled over at her. "Besides, he'd do almost anything for a pretty lady."

Her pulse picked up, and her stomach flipped again. She silently scolded herself. It was a general statement, not aimed specifically at her.

She brushed the unwanted flutters aside and helped him turn the boat over. He had said his shoulder was healing well, but his arm was still in the sling. She wasn't going to chance him tearing something.

He began using the towel to dry off the hull and wipe away any clinging sand. "If we run the duct tape over the gunnel, around the hull and back over the other side, that should hold it until we get back."

She took the towel from him and shook the sand from it, then dropped to her knees to resume wiping down the hull. She was determined to stay busy. Because as long as she kept her focus on the task at hand, it wouldn't allow room for other thoughts.

Such as how Blake's accusation filled her head with all kinds of impossible dreams.

And how Hunter's admission sent both hope and dread surging through her at the same time.

And how, no matter how much she tried not to, she couldn't help wondering what it would be like to be loved by a man like Hunter.

SIX

Hunter cruised down Fifth Street, windows open. The noonday air was warm, but not uncomfortably so. Besides, the wind on his face felt good. Maybe the fresh air would help to blow some of the cobwebs from his brain.

He needed to get his head back on straight, something that wasn't likely to happen while he was seeing Meagan almost every day. Just six weeks ago, life had seemed simple. He had his job, his boys Sunday school class and his volunteer work with the Cedar Key National Wildlife Refuge. And few outside distractions.

Then he'd met Meagan Berry, and she'd turned his ordered life upside down.

She was a bundle of contradictions. She was strong and self-sufficient enough to roll up her sleeves and change a flat tire, but possessed an underlying vulnerability that reached right in and grabbed him by the heart. She was brave enough to fake her own death and travel all the way across the country to escape her psycho ex-fiancé, but mentally shut down when faced with his anger.

Except yesterday, on Snake Key. He'd been so upset with her for putting herself in danger, he had wanted to shake her. Instead, he had just yelled at her. And she had stood up to him and yelled right back. Maybe she'd felt more confident with Blake there. Or maybe she was starting to see that he was different from the other men she had known, that she had no reason to fear him. That no matter what happened, he would never, ever lay an abusive hand on a woman.

Now he had to pick her up for work. Today's hours were one to six. And whether the damage was done to her boat six weeks ago or the day before yesterday, he wasn't willing to let her go anywhere alone.

As he pulled into Meagan's driveway, Sydney Tanner waved at him from the end of the road. She held a leash, its other end attached to her dachshund, Chandler. As soon as he stepped from the cruiser, she held up an envelope and called to him.

"I have mail for Meagan."

She picked up her pace, hurrying toward him. Chandler broke into a run in front of her, ears flopping and stubby little legs a blur. They took a diagonal path through Meagan's front yard and met him at the truck.

"This was in my mailbox. When I saw Meagan's name and address on it, I figured the mailman put it in the wrong box. But it's not stamped."

Hunter took the envelope and looked at its front. Meagan's name and address were printed in the center, but other than that, it was blank. There was no return address, no postage stamp.

Uneasiness crept along his spine. This wasn't delivered by the postman. Someone had chosen a random box a block away, where he could leave it unobserved. And he would know that, in a small town like Cedar Key, where everyone knew everyone else, chances were good the envelope would get to its addressee.

Pressure against his pant leg drew Hunter's attention downward. Chandler stood staring up at him, front paw raised and tail wagging. Hunter slid the envelope into his shirt pocket and squatted to scratch the dog's neck and cheeks. The tail picked up speed, and the long, pink tongue shot in and out, bathing both of his palms and forearms.

The front door to the house swung open, and Meagan stepped out. She was smiling, and there was a softness in her eyes. "You must like dogs."

"I like animals, period. All kinds." He straightened, and Sydney bade them farewell to finish Chandler's middle-of-the-day walk.

Hunter pulled the envelope from his pocket and showed it to Meagan. "Sydney stopped to deliver a piece of mail that was left in her box."

Furrows settled between Meagan's brows. She had apparently noticed the lack of a stamp and return address.

"I'm sure if there were any prints left on the envelope, they would be destroyed, since Sydney carried it all the way here from her box, then handed it to me. But I don't want to handle the contents without gloves."

He went to the patrol car and pulled a pair of latex ones from the trunk. Once he'd removed and unfolded the page, Meagan read the words aloud, her voice as thin as the paper from which she was reading.

"Why won't you die? He's no longer here, so you don't deserve to be, either."

Hunter stepped closer so he could put his arm across her shoulders, and then pulled her closer still. A head shorter than his six feet, her small frame fit well against his side, and he wanted to wrap her in his arms and shield her from whatever danger was out there. She had finally gotten a reprieve. It had lasted less than two weeks.

She leaned into him, accepting the comfort he was offering. "He's back." Her voice was still weak, with a slight waver. "Or maybe he never left. Maybe that white sedan had nothing to do with me."

"Either way, we've got to stay on guard." Hunter looked around them, across the street, up and down Fifth, between the houses. Someone could have them in his sights at that very moment, aiming, preparing to take a shot.

"Let's get in the car. It's not safe to stand outside." He led her to the passenger's side and helped her in, then circled around to get behind the wheel. After he had backed out of her driveway and started down Fifth, he looked over at her. Her eyes were closed, and her head was resting against the seat. But the tight jaw and firm grip on the armrest told him that she wasn't relaxed.

He reached across and covered her hand with his. "We'll catch him. Now that he's back, we'll set a trap. It's just a matter of time till he makes a mistake and someone sees him."

She opened her eyes and let her head roll to the side until she was facing him. "In the meantime, I go back to being a prisoner."

"If you get to where you can't stand it anymore and just have to get away, we'll all go with you—Blake, Joe and me." He smiled over at her, summoning a cheer he didn't feel. "We can even take the tour over to Seahorse Key, let you pretend you're a tourist."

She frowned, and her eyes darkened. "Seahorse Key doesn't hold the appeal that it once did. I can't get the plane crash out of my mind, the fact that I wasn't able to save the pilot. I know it's silly. I know he was already dead, that there wasn't anything I could do for him. But

I keep seeing the water creeping up his face, covering his mouth, his nose…"

She closed her eyes, and a shudder shook her shoulders. Hunter squeezed her hand, then eased to a stop in front of Darci's store and shifted into Park. But Meagan made no move to get out.

"I think the image has haunted me so much because of my fear of the water. It started when I was six. We were over at some friends' house having a cookout. Mom was pregnant with my sister and it was hot, so she was inside in the air-conditioning. My dad was helping his friend man the grill, but they had been drinking for the last hour and were getting pretty wasted. My mom had warned me to stay away from the pool, but my friend convinced me to go inside the gate with her. Then she thought it would be funny to push me in."

"Great friend."

"She was five and had been swimming since she was two. So she didn't know any better. Anyway, they almost didn't get me out in time. I had stopped breathing, and they had to do CPR. Ever since, I've been terrified of drowning."

"But you've learned to swim."

She gave him a weak smile. There was a touch of pride in it. "Yes, I did. Edmund knew I couldn't swim, knew how terrified I was of the water. So I figured if I could secretly learn, I could use my new skill to escape, and he would never suspect. So I watched YouTube videos and practiced in the pool when neither Edmund nor Lou were around."

"That's pretty impressive." Not just the fact that she was able to forge ahead through her fear, but the fact that she'd done it alone. The more Hunter learned about Meagan, the more he admired her. She was a special

lady. After all she'd been through, she deserved someone who appreciated her spunk and talent and concern
for others, someone who would love and respect her, and
treat her with care and tenderness.

But he wasn't that man.

He reached across to squeeze her shoulder. "I'm sorry
you had to witness that. But don't beat yourself up. There
was nothing you could have done. Even if the impact
hadn't killed him, you would have only had time to save
one."

"I would have had to choose who lived and who died.
That would have been horrible." She managed another
weak smile. "I guess no matter what happens, it could
have always been worse. At least he was already gone."

She stepped from the car and, after thanking him for
the ride, closed the door. As he pulled away from the
curb, her words circled through his mind: *At least he
was already gone.*

Was there someone who didn't know that? Was there
some girlfriend or family member of the pilot who
blamed Meagan for not trying to save him? Maybe all
the death threats had nothing to do with Charlie. Maybe
the source was much closer than California. Maybe it
had all started right here in Cedar Key.

Hunter turned the car around and headed toward the
police station. The first thing he would do was get the
autopsy report. The final one wouldn't be ready for some
time yet, but the department could request a preliminary.

Then, regardless of what the autopsy showed, they
would do some investigation into the pilot's life. Every
family member, any romantic interests, each friend.
Anyone who'd had anything to do with the man for the
past year.

Hunter pulled into the small parking area in front of

the police station. This afternoon, they would pass his ideas on to Levy County. And they would work together to get this thing solved.

As he swung open the glass door and stepped inside, a weight lifted from his shoulders. He drew in a long, unimpeded breath and straightened his spine.

After more a month of searching for answers, he had finally come up with something that made sense.

Mouthwatering aromas filled the air—eggs, bacon, sausages and hotcakes—along with the clinking of silverware against porcelain and the hum of a dozen conversations. Ken's Cedar Keyside Diner was busy this morning. With its fun, casual atmosphere and fantastic breakfasts, Ken's was busy most mornings.

Hunter drew in a fragrant breath, and his stomach rumbled. Two meals were on their way. Meagan had chosen an Oldsmobile Omelet, and after some deliberation, he had gone with the Packard Omelet. There were also the Chevy Meals and the Autobahn Delights to choose from. The Blown Engine Meal was beyond his capabilities—it could serve a small army.

Meagan smiled over at him. "You could have just run me by The Market to restock on eggs and milk."

"We'll do that on the way home tonight. You have to admit, this is way more fun than breakfast by yourself." Having Meagan's company was always more fun than eating alone.

Before she could respond, his cell phone started to ring. He swiped the screen and pressed it to his ear. It was Detective Gorman with Levy County. As Gorman began to relay what he had learned, Hunter's pulse picked up and hope spiked through him. He had told Meagan of his suspicions that the threats might be re-

lated to the death of the pilot. Based on Gorman's information, chances were good that he was right.

By the time he disconnected the call several minutes
later, Meagan was leaning toward him, eyes wide and
body rigid with anticipation. He slid the phone back into
its case and watched the waitress approach. Meagan
would have to wait a few seconds longer.

After blessing the food and spreading a napkin in
his lap, Hunter locked eyes with her. "That was Levy
County. And it looks like we're finally getting somewhere."

"Really?" Meagan's anticipation had turned to excitement.

"Yep. The pilot didn't have a current wife or girlfriend. And neither of his two exes seemed upset enough
about his death to go after you for it. But the detectives
uncovered some pretty interesting things about the pilot's sister."

He picked up his fork and cut off the end of his omelet. "The name's Sally Ferguson. She's had a lot of
mental problems over the years. They started showing
up when she was thirteen. At sixteen, she had a tiff with
her best friend, a fight over a guy."

Meagan took a swig of orange juice and smiled. "Isn't
that usually what sixteen-year-old girls fight over?"

"You've got a point. Except in this case, the friend
turned up dead."

"Whoa, that's a pretty serious disagreement. Did they
charge Sally with it?"

"No. The girl drowned in Sally's family's pool. Her
blood-alcohol level was almost double the legal limit
for driving. Everyone knew the two of them were at
odds, fighting over this guy. But Sally claimed that her
friend was having some problems with him and needed

a girl to talk to. The two of them got into Sally's dad's liquor stash. Apparently once the friend got started, she wouldn't stop. Sally claimed her friend got really inebriated, then fell into the pool."

"That sounds legitimate."

"Except that there was some bruising around the dead girl's neck and shoulders. And Sally had scratch marks on her arms."

"*That* sounds suspicious."

"Yeah, that's what the investigators thought." He took another bite of omelet before continuing. "But Sally claimed that she had dived in to try to save her, and the drowning girl panicked and fought her, like drowning people often do. The investigation pretty much stopped there. Either the evidence was too inconclusive, or her dad kept it from going any further. He was some big-time lawyer with deep pockets."

"Any other run-ins with the law? Or add-on bodies?"

"That was it as far as suspicious deaths. But over the next couple of years, her mental condition deteriorated, and she was in and out of hospitals. For the past decade, she's been under the care of the pilot. He made sure she took her meds the way she was supposed to, and she apparently functioned pretty well. But for the past month and a half, she's been on her own. I'm betting she hasn't touched a pill since that plane went down."

"You're probably right."

He picked up a knife and spread some jelly on his toast. "Guess what she drives."

"A white sedan with tinted windows."

"Yep, a Cadillac DeVille."

"Any pink paint?"

"No. But she could have had it touched up. Or maybe it didn't leave any, especially since the bike was probably already lying down when she ran over it. We actually had checked out the car previously. It was one of the three with plates beginning 56Y. We didn't make the connection to the pilot, though, because the last name was different. Sally Ferguson is Bruce Jennings's half sister. Same mother, different fathers."

"Wow." Meagan wiped her mouth with her napkin and shook her head. "All this time I've been thinking about Charlie, wondering how someone connected with him could have found me in Cedar Key."

"Yeah, me, too."

"So where does Sally live?"

"At her brother's place in Fanning Springs." At Meagan's raised brow, he continued. "It's a little town at the northernmost edge of Levy County. At this very moment, we're waiting for a warrant to search the place. Gorman's going to let me know, and I'll head there once I drop you off at work."

Meagan finished the last of her omelet and sat back in her chair. "I can't believe this might be over soon." A relaxed smile climbed up her cheeks and settled in her eyes. "It's going to feel so good to have my life back. And I have you to thank."

"Me and a bunch of other people."

"But you're the one who has stuck by me the closest, above and beyond the call of duty." Her eyes filled with admiration. "You're a good man, Hunter Kingston."

"And you're a special lady."

She gave him a rueful smile. "I'm a mess."

He reached across the table and took her hand. "With everything you've been through in the past year, you have every right to be a mess. But you're not. You're amazing." And if he wasn't careful, he was going to find himself caring for her much more than he should.

The waitress approached with their check, and he pulled back his hand. After paying the bill, he walked Meagan to the door. The moment they stepped into the crisp morning air, a notification sounded on his phone. It was a text from Gorman, short and sweet—We have the warrant—followed by an address.

Meagan climbed into his truck, excitement radiating from her. "Let me know what you find out."

"I will." He closed the door and circled around to the driver's side. He was supposed to be off today. But they were possibly on the verge of their big break. And he wouldn't miss it for anything.

He eased to a stop in front of Darci's store and watched Meagan enter before pulling away from the curb. There was one thing he hadn't told her, something he would never tell her.

Yesterday they'd received the preliminary autopsy report. And it wasn't at all what he had expected. The pilot didn't die from injuries sustained in the crash. True, he had a broken neck, but that wasn't what had killed him. He had drowned.

Hearing the news was like having a bucket of ice water dumped over his head. He couldn't tell Meagan. If she learned the truth, she would be devastated.

When he pulled up to the address Levy County had given him, the detectives were at the door, warrant in hand. This was no little cabin in the woods. It was an impressive two-story house situated on an acre or two right on the river. The pilot obviously had had some money. Or maybe it was his daddy's money. At any rate, he had lived well.

Hunter stepped from the car and approached the house. The three-car garage was to the left, the top quarter of each door sporting a row of windows.

He peeked inside. The white sedan was there. So was a red Ford Explorer. A sticker on the bumper of the SUV said I'd Rather Be Flying, and there was a Browning deer hunting logo on the back window.

His pulse picked up speed. He knew that Explorer. He had seen it around town, driven by a woman, if he remembered correctly. After trying to run over Meagan, she had apparently kept the sedan hidden and found a way back home, maybe took a cab. All while they had been looking for a white sedan, Sally Ferguson had been moving freely about town in a Ford Explorer.

None of the management companies on Cedar Key had a record of her renting a house or condo. He had checked yesterday. But that didn't mean anything. She could have checked in under an assumed name and paid cash. Or rented from an individual.

Hunter moved toward the front door. As he stepped onto the porch, the two detectives turned around. He introduced himself, although it wasn't necessary. They had communicated via phone several times during the past three days.

Detective Gorman tilted his head toward the door. "She's not answering. We may have to enter forcibly."

Hunter nodded. "The sedan is in the garage, along with a red Ford Explorer that I know I've seen around Cedar Key over the past couple of weeks."

Detective Franklin frowned. "When we talked to her a few weeks ago, she insisted that she hadn't been to Cedar Key in years. Obviously, she was lying."

After finding all the doors locked, Franklin kicked in the front one and the three of them entered, weapons drawn. Hunter crept through the house with the detectives as they cleared each room, his senses on full alert. Chances

YOUR PARTICIPATION IS REQUESTED!

Dear Reader,

Since you are a lover of our books – we would like to get to know you!

Inside you will find a short Reader's Survey. Sharing your answers with us will help our editorial staff understand who you are and what activities you enjoy.

To thank you for your participation, we would like to send you 2 books and 2 gifts – **ABSOLUTELY FREE!**

Enjoy your gifts with our appreciation,

Pam Powers

SEE INSIDE FOR READER'S SURVEY

For Your Reading Pleasure...

We'll send you 2 books and 2 gifts
ABSOLUTELY FREE
just for completing our Reader's Survey!

YOUR READER'S SURVEY
"THANK YOU" FREE GIFTS INCLUDE:
▶ **2 FREE books**
▶ **2 lovely surprise gifts**

PLEASE FILL IN THE CIRCLES COMPLETELY TO RESPOND

1) What type of fiction books do you enjoy reading? (Check all that apply)
- ○ Suspense/Thrillers
- ○ Action/Adventure
- ○ Modern-day Romances
- ○ Historical Romance
- ○ Humour
- ○ Paranormal Romance

2) What attracted you most to the last fiction book you purchased on impulse?
- ○ The Title
- ○ The Cover
- ○ The Author
- ○ The Story

3) What is usually the greatest influencer when you <u>plan</u> to buy a book?
- ○ Advertising
- ○ Referral
- ○ Book Review

4) How often do you access the internet?
- ○ Daily ○ Weekly ○ Monthly ○ Rarely or never.

5) How many NEW paperback fiction novels have you purchased in the past 3 months?
- ○ 0 - 2
- ○ 3 - 6
- ○ 7 or more

YES! I have completed the Reader's Survey. Please send me the 2 FREE books and 2 FREE gifts (gifts are worth about $10) for which I qualify. I understand that I am under no obligation to purchase any books, as explained on the back of this card.

❑ I prefer the regular-print edition
153/353 IDL GH6A

❑ I prefer the larger-print edition
107/307 IDL GH6A

FIRST NAME	LAST NAME

ADDRESS

APT.#	CITY

STATE/PROV.	ZIP/POSTAL CODE

SLI-515-SUR15

were good that she was gone. But he wasn't counting on it. She was dangerous. He knew that firsthand.

Once certain they were alone, the detectives spread out, going in different directions. Hunter chose his own. Off the side of the foyer was a den. He'd gotten a brief look when Gorman checked the room on first entering.

He pushed open the massive double doors and stepped inside. This was Bruce Jennings's space, definitely a man cave—from the dark walnut paneling, to the large mahogany desk and other heavy furniture, to the half-dozen deer heads mounted on the walls, trophies from hunting trips.

But what snagged his gaze and held it was the impressive collection of bows and arrows on display. Some were simple archery bows, made of gracefully curved wood, a grip and a taut bowstring. Others were metal crossbows, much more complicated. And much more lethal. Capable of killing someone with the pull of a trigger.

In the center of one wall was an empty hook. One bow was missing—likely the weapon that had fired the shot intended to kill Meagan. His right hand went to his shoulder. Two and a half weeks had passed, and as long as he didn't lift his arm, he was doing well. He hardly knew he'd been injured, except for occasional twinges. And a nasty red scar. If Sally Ferguson was the expert archer her brother had been, Meagan would be dead.

Now they had two obvious things linking Sally to the attempts on Meagan's life—the white sedan and a missing crossbow. A bottle of cyanide would seal the case up tight.

He moved to the other side of the room, where an oak gun cabinet stood against the wall. Although it wasn't full, an array of rifles and shotguns were displayed in the wide center portion, and several pistols occupied the two narrower side sections. The glass doors were locked. But that didn't mean Sally didn't have a key. Chances were good that she did. And had already armed herself.

Hunter had just stepped into the foyer when Detective Franklin's voice came from the back of the house. "Hey, Gorman, Kingston."

When he entered the kitchen, Franklin was holding a jar in one latex-covered hand. "I found this under the sink."

Hunter raised a brow. "Cyanide?"

"The label says sodium ferrocyanide." The detective unscrewed the lid and tilted the jar. It was half empty. Yellow crystalline granules filled the bottom.

"What is it?" Hunter was no chemist, but cyanide in the name didn't sound good.

"Not exactly cyanide." Gorman squatted to look under the sink. "But it can be used to make cyanide." He stood moments later, holding a canister. "Sodium carbonate, for adjusting a pool's pH. It's available at any pool supply store. Combine it with sodium ferrocyanide in the right proportions, heat it up and you have almost pure cyanide. There are a few more steps than that, but you get the gist."

"I think we have a pretty good idea of who made the cyanide-laced brownies." Franklin's tone was serious.

They didn't find anything else while searching the rest of the house. But they didn't need to. With a pool out back, Sally Ferguson would be expected to have sodium carbonate. But the average homeowner had no reason to be in possession of a jar of sodium ferrocyanide. Combined with her access to a wide assortment of bows, one of which was missing, and the fact that she owned a car fitting the description of the one that had almost hit Meagan, Hunter had no doubt they had identified Meagan's stalker. They would swear out a warrant for her arrest and watch the house until she was caught.

As he walked into the afternoon sun with Gorman and Franklin, relief swept over him, even excitement. They had done it. They had solved the case. He could hardly wait to call Meagan.

But as he got into his truck, a sudden dose of reality punched him in the chest. Soon Sally Ferguson would no longer be a threat.

But Edmund was still out there. And Edmund wanted her dead just as surely as Sally did. Maybe he wasn't as immediate a threat. Maybe the tough guy who had come to Nature's Landing and questioned Anna really had been a reporter.

But whatever Meagan did, wherever she went, there was always the chance that someday Edmund would find her. That knowledge was like an ominous black cloud. Although it seemed farther away at times, it never really lifted.

As long as Edmund was still out there, Meagan would never be truly free.

SEVEN

Meagan put a piece of key lime pie into her mouth and closed her eyes, savoring the tangy sweetness. Hunter had thought that, since they had finally identified her stalker, it was time to celebrate. She had insisted that their celebration was premature and should wait until Sally Ferguson was actually apprehended. Hunter won the argument.

So here they were, for the second time that day, sitting across the table from each other. This time it was at the Island Hotel Restaurant, one of Cedar Key's finest dining establishments. Dessert plates sat in front of them, and a candle flickered in the middle of the table. The quaint setting, the dim lighting and the soft music playing in the background contributed to the romantic atmosphere. So much so that Meagan had to keep telling herself there was no romance between her and Hunter. With each reminder, disappointment stabbed through her.

She hadn't wanted to fall for him. She hadn't wanted to fall for anyone. But from the moment he'd pulled her out of the water after the plane crash, their lives had become inextricably bound. And no matter how she fought to hold on to her resolve, every time she saw the concern in those blue eyes, the wall she had placed around her heart got a little thinner, until now there was nothing left.

She swallowed the bite she had just taken, and smiled at Hunter. Their dinner conversation had spanned all kinds of topics, the last of which was his sister, Amber. Before that, they had covered everything from their childhoods, to their likes and dislikes, to life in Cedar Key. Everything except Edmund and Sally Ferguson. Hunter had probably planned it that way. And she was grateful. The evening had been a true escape.

He sliced into a piece of hot apple pie. "Amber's planning to spend a few days here next month."

"Will she stay with you?"

"I hope not." He laughed. "She's coming with three friends. Four women in my small two-bedroom house would be estrogen overload." He once again grew serious. "When she comes, I'll introduce you. She would like you."

Meagan's heart fluttered at the thought of Hunter introducing her to his family. Then she silently scolded herself. Introducing his sister to his friends when she came to visit wasn't the same as bringing the new girlfriend to meet the parents. Far from it.

"So I assume it's just you and Amber, right? No other siblings?"

His gaze dipped to the table before he answered. "No, I have a twin brother."

"Really? Where is he?" His sister had come up in conversation a couple times, but he had never mentioned having a brother.

"Starke." Disdain underscored the word. Or maybe it was embarrassment.

"Starke?"

He met her eyes. "Florida State Prison."

"Hey, almost every family has someone who has ended up on the wrong side of the law. It's not a big deal."

He scowled at her. "I'm a cop, and I have a brother who's doing fifteen years."

"That's still no reflection on you." She speared her last piece of pie and put it into her mouth. "So who's older, you guys or Amber?"

"We are, by five years."

"I'm the older child, too, by six years. My sister and I had our issues, but if anybody picked on her, I was all over them." She started to smile at the fond memories. Then a pang of homesickness shot through her, turning that warmth into searing pain.

Hunter's eyes filled with tenderness. "I can tell you miss her. Someday you'll be with her again. Your mom, too. Don't give up hope."

Meagan nodded. "When I see Darci with her mom, I feel so homesick for my own I can hardly stand it. But I'm glad Darci has her, especially now."

"How is she doing with getting Jayden into a program?"

Meagan frowned. "That's a good question. She had an appointment with someone Friday afternoon, but we were so busy at the store this morning, we never got a chance to talk about it. Then she left, and I was by myself this afternoon."

"I'll see her in church tomorrow." Hunter took a sip of the coffee that the waitress had just refilled. "Why don't you join us? We can give *him* a break." He tilted his head toward the undercover detective who sat two tables away. He was just starting what looked like a slice of some kind of chocolate decadence.

She smiled. "Right now he's probably not minding this assignment too much."

"You're probably right. At least this part of it. Hanging out in Darci's store all day or hiding in your neighbor's bushes isn't nearly as pleasant. But I suppose you have to take the good with the bad." Hunter scooped up another bite of apple pie. "So what do you say?"

She lifted her brows. "About what?"

"Going to church with me."

"Thanks, but I think I'll pass."

"Come on, it's got to beat sitting at home, bored."

"I don't get bored. I read, I draw, I paint. I've never had time for boredom." She took a sip of coffee, its warmth soothing. Something had been bothering her ever since learning of Jayden's diagnosis. "I'm a little upset at God right now."

"Why? What did God do to you?"

"It's not what He did to me. It's what He *didn't* do for somebody who really deserved it."

"Darci," he answered immediately. The man was perceptive, if nothing else.

She leaned back in her chair and sighed. "During the time she was waiting for Jayden's test results, she was praying so hard for the diagnosis to come back good. I know her mom was praying, and you were, and she said everyone at church was, too."

She drew in a deep breath. "Darci's such a good person. She's always giving of herself. Those middle school girls she teaches adore her. It's obvious every time one of them comes into the store. You don't get that kind of love and respect unless you give it. And no matter what she says, I know she offered me this job because I was at the end of my rope, not because she really needed me." She set down her fork and crossed her arms. "If anyone deserves to have their prayers answered, it's Darci. But God ignored her. And I think that just stinks."

"God never ignores His children. Sometimes we don't get the answers we want. But the answer is always there, along with the strength to face whatever lies ahead. God has given Darci that strength. You can see she hasn't buckled under this."

No, she hadn't. Just the opposite. She seemed to be facing the whole situation with a calm confidence that frankly didn't make sense.

But Darci was strong. She had the responsibility of her business, as well as raising a son. She had never mentioned Jayden's father, but he clearly wasn't involved in her or Jayden's lives. So she was on her own. With the diagnosis, the job of raising a child alone got a whole lot harder. But she wasn't falling apart. Yes, Darci had strength enough for ten women.

Was that strength innate? A basic part of her personality? Or was she drawing from something outside of herself, a higher power?

Hunter leaned toward her, his gaze earnest. "God doesn't promise to keep us from trouble. But He does promise to walk with us through it. To give us peace in the midst of the storm."

Peace in the midst of the storm. Was it really possible? She had endured a lot of storms during her life. But over the past year, they had been full-blown hurricanes. And they weren't done yet. She could use some of that peace Hunter was talking about.

"I'll think about it. Probably not tomorrow, but maybe another week." She laid her cloth napkin on the table and stood. "I'm going to go to the restroom before we head home."

As she made her way out of the dining room, her eyes fell on a table in the corner. A woman sat there alone, a hardcover book open in front of her. She glanced up from her reading as Meagan passed. Although the woman offered her a smile, it didn't reach her eyes. Instead there was something else there, an odd sort of intensity.

Meagan shook off the sense of uneasiness that trickled over her and continued toward the restrooms. The only threat to her life right now was Sally Ferguson. Hunter had shown her pictures, and the lone woman sitting in the corner wasn't her. Sally carried an extra twenty or thirty pounds, and her auburn hair was short, tapering to a point on each side at her jawline. The woman in the restaurant had long blond hair, and if she had excess fat on her body anywhere, she was doing a great job of hiding it.

While Meagan was inside the stall, the bathroom door creaked open. The same uneasiness she had felt when passing by the woman slid over her again. She brushed it aside. She was in a restaurant, a public place. Chances were good she wouldn't have the restroom to herself.

Heels clicked against the wood floor, and the lock in the adjoining stall slid into position. Some of the tension left Meagan's body. Just a patron of the restaurant here for the same reason she was. She exited the stall and turned on the water at the sink.

As she reached for the soap, the other stall door opened. It was the blonde from the corner table. She carried a purse over her shoulder, one of those oversize bags so popular now.

When Meagan met her gaze in the mirror, coldness spread through her core. If hatred could be expressed through nothing more than the eyes, this woman had mastered the art. She walked straight to the door, reaching into her bag as she went. But instead of pulling the door open, she twisted the lock.

Meagan stiffened and drew in a sharp breath. A single scream would have both Hunter and the undercover detective kicking in the door.

But she never got the opportunity. When the woman turned, she held a pistol in her hand. And pointed it at Meagan's chest.

"You make a peep, and you'll get a bullet right through your heart."

Meagan held up both hands. "You don't want to do that. There are two law enforcement officers in the next room. If you fire that weapon, there's no chance you'll walk out of here."

The woman threw back her head and laughed, the sound full of contempt. "I fire this weapon and no one will know until someone walks in here and finds you dead in your own blood."

Meagan's eyes dipped to the gun. Something was attached to the end of the barrel. Probably a silencer.

"What do you want? Money? I don't have any on me. I left my purse at the table." Even as the words tumbled out, she knew. She wasn't being mugged. She was locked in the bathroom with Sally Ferguson. She'd been duped. They all had. Because Sally didn't look at all like her pictures.

She wore thick-rimmed glasses, and she had lost weight, at least twenty pounds, probably more. And her hair was all wrong. It was obviously a wig. Meagan silently scolded herself. She shouldn't have been so easily fooled. She was a master of disguises herself.

Her thoughts spun, ticking through her options. Sally wanted her dead and would have no qualms about shooting her and letting her die on the bathroom floor. If there was any chance of making it though this night alive, she would have to go along with whatever the woman wanted. And keep ever alert for any opportunity to escape.

Sally made a quick motion with the gun. "Over there, against the wall." She moved to the window and opened the blinds. "Turn around. You try anything and you're dead."

Meagan turned to face the wall. A moment later the lock clicked, and wood scraped against wood as the window slid up in its track. Her blood turned to ice. Was Sally going to shoot her in the back, then escape through the window?

"All right. Now climb out. And hurry up."

The breath she'd been holding spilled out in a relieved sigh. She crossed the small bathroom and put her head through the window. It opened onto the hotel's patio garden. No one was there. Of course, Sally had probably already checked that out.

Meagan raised one leg and swung it through the opening. Several seconds later, she dropped to the ground and surveyed her surroundings. Wrought-iron tables and chairs sat on the brick pavers. An abundance of plants softened the area, and palm trees grew near one wall. A wooden gate opened onto Second Street. If she could make it out the gate…

Sally pointed the gun through the opening. "Don't even think about running. I'm a good shot. You'll never outrun my bullet."

Meagan hesitated. The sun had set some time ago, but it wasn't dark. An almost-full moon shone down, assisted by two strings of lights draping the perimeter of the garden. If Sally's pistol skills were like her skills with a crossbow, Meagan might stand a chance. But she wouldn't risk her life to find out.

Sally negotiated the window easily and joined her within moments.

"Now we're going to walk. I'm putting the gun in the bag. But I can have it back out in two seconds flat. So don't get any ideas."

Sally led her out the gate, then through a series of left turns until they were headed west on Third. It was less traveled than Second. But up ahead, a couple moved toward them, walking hand in hand.

Sally leaned closer. "If you even think about trying to get their help, they die first, so you can watch. And then you die."

Hopelessness descended on her. The farther she got from downtown, the less chance she had of surviving the night. She squared her shoulders. Maybe she *would* die tonight. But she wasn't going to be responsible for innocent people losing their lives.

The couple passed them, and she waited to speak until they were out of hearing range. "Why are you doing this? What have I done?"

"You know what you did. You were there and didn't even try to save him."

"I saw the plane go down. But when I motored out there, your brother was already dead."

"No, he wasn't. He was still alive, and you let him drown. You chose to save the senator and let my brother die."

"He was dead. His neck was broken."

"It was broken, but you could have saved him."

"How?"

"Gotten him out of the plane the way you did the senator. Instead, you let him drown."

"He didn't drown." She kept her tone low and soothing, even though frustration was now melding with the fear. "He was already dead when I got there."

Sally suddenly stopped walking and reached into her purse. Meagan's heart leaped into her throat. But the woman didn't pull out the gun. Instead, she handed her a sheet of paper.

"What's this?"

"An autopsy report."

Meagan dropped her eyes to the page, illuminated by a nearby streetlight. A sick sense of dread filled her gut as her eyes sought out the line "Cause of death."

No, she didn't want to read it. She wanted to keep believing that he was already gone when she arrived, that there was nothing she could have done.

But she could no longer deny the truth. Because it was right in front of her—cause of death: drowning. Her blood turned to ice, chilling her all the way to her soul.

"No." The paper slid from her hand and fluttered to the sidewalk. She took several slow steps backward. "He was gone when I got there. His head was so far to the side, there was no way he could have survived."

Sally scooped up the report and stuffed it back into her purse. "You can't deny what you just read yourself."

No, she couldn't. While the water slowly climbed up the pilot's face, he'd been alive. Still breathing. "I'm so sorry. I didn't know. But there wasn't time." If she would have just worked a little more quickly...

"You say there wasn't time, but you took the time to get the senator out. You chose him, because he was someone important."

Meagan shook her head. "No, I didn't know who he was."

"I don't believe you. His face is always on the news."

"Not in California. I had just moved to Florida. I didn't know who he was."

"It doesn't matter. You let my brother die. Now walk, before I shoot you right here on the sidewalk."

Meagan dropped her gaze to her feet and willed them to move. She finally managed it, each footstep taking her closer to her death. No words would come. Her mind had shut down.

All the way down Third Street, they didn't encounter another person. Third ended at G, which ran along the Gulf. When they reached it, Sally guided her to turn right.

Toward Darci's parents' house. Where Meagan kept her boat.

"Where are we going?"

"For a ride."

"In my boat?" Fear had constricted her throat, making her question come out in a high-pitched squeak. "But it's not fixed. The three holes are still there. They need to be patched."

"I checked the tape. It'll hold up just fine."

Yes, it probably would. And the motor was fixed. Hunter had seen to that.

He had thought he was doing her a favor.

Instead, he had hastened her demise.

Hunter looked at his watch for the fourth time in the past ten minutes. He had already asked for the check, paid and gotten his credit card back. And Meagan still hadn't returned to the table. Another woman had gone into the restroom after her, a woman with long blond hair. Probably a tourist, since he hadn't seen her around. Since neither of them had emerged, they had apparently struck up a conversation. And judging from the length of time that had passed, they were working on giving each other their life histories.

He shook his head. Men just didn't do things like that, especially in restrooms.

He swallowed the last of his coffee, which was now lukewarm. Maybe he should knock on the door. He didn't want to rush her. If she'd found some lady that she really connected with, and they wanted to have a lengthy conversation in a restaurant bathroom, more power to 'em. But he was starting to grow concerned.

When he rose from the table, the detective looked his way. Hunter gave him a slight nod. He didn't need him yet but wanted him on alert, just in case.

Hunter stopped at the door marked Ladies and gave a couple raps. Several moments passed in silence. His concern ratcheted up a dozen notches. He knocked again. "Meagan?" Still silence.

When he tried the doorknob, it wouldn't turn. It was locked from the inside. Panic gripped him. He shook it, then banged hard on the door. "Meagan!"

A footfall sounded, and he spun in time to see the detective step up next to him.

"The door's locked."

Restaurant management probably had a key. Hunter wasn't going to wait that long. He stepped back, then thrust his foot out. The door sprang inward, revealing a broken jamb.

And an empty restroom.

The window was open. The screen, if there had been one, was missing. He crossed the small space to put his head through the opening. The patio area was empty. Meagan was gone. And Sally Ferguson had her.

Hunter's mind fractured, his thoughts scattering in a thousand different directions. He spun to address the detective, but he had stepped into the hall and was already on his phone.

They had been duped. The woman sitting alone in the corner had been Sally. The disguise was a good one. Not only had she hidden her short hair beneath a long blond wig, she had somehow managed to shed a lot of weight since the pictures they had were taken. And she had slipped Meagan out, right under their noses.

Hunter dashed from the building, the detective right behind him, and looked both ways on Second Street. Several people strolled down the sidewalk. None of them were Meagan or Sally. But he wasn't giving up. Someone had to have seen something. He would talk to everyone he could. Sally would be easily remembered with the wig—waist length, thick and beautiful. It was the kind of hair people noticed.

The detective ended the call and pocketed his phone. "We've got backup coming, both Cedar Key and Levy County. We'll all be combing the island for them. And there's going to be a roadblock set up. There's no way she'll be able to slip past us."

Hunter drew in a calming breath. The detective was right. There was only one route back to the mainland. But what if Sally didn't try to leave? What if she just decided to kill Meagan on Cedar Key? His heart twisted in his chest. No, she couldn't die. They had to find her.

The first several people he talked to were no help. Then a young couple mentioned seeing two women fitting their description moving down Third Street toward the water. Maybe Sally had her vehicle waiting. Maybe she was at that moment preparing to make her way off Cedar Key.

And right into the trap set up by Levy County.

After thanking the couple, he jogged back to his

truck. When he reached the end of Third, he glanced left, then right, down G Street. It was deserted. Houses lined the street, but apparently everyone was already inside for the night. The likelihood that anyone had seen anything was slim.

He took a right on G and pulled into a drive. He would knock on some doors and find out what he could. Then he would do what other law enforcement was doing, combing the streets, hoping to stop Sally before it was too late. He stepped from the truck and started up the driveway.

Two doors down was the Tucker place. They would be shocked to learn what had happened. They liked Meagan. Besides seeing her at the store on a regular basis, they were in frequent contact because she kept her boat in their backyard.

Meagan's boat. Dread washed through him and settled in his gut. Was that where Sally had taken her?

Leaving his truck, he sprinted toward the Tuckers' yard, then slipped between the two houses. A pole light illuminated the dock, along with the small patch of beach where Meagan's boat always sat.

It was gone.

Sally had kidnapped her and taken her away on Meagan's own boat. There was a roadblock set up to catch her if she tried to leave Cedar Key. But Sally had outsmarted them again. She hadn't gone by land. She had gone by water, planning to bypass them all.

He reached for his phone. The Cedar Key Fire rescue boat could be in the water in minutes. So could his own. And Blake's was already there, moored at the marina.

While making the two phone calls, Hunter hurried back to his truck. He would head home and hook up his boat. Then would come an almost hopeless search—

finding one small johnboat on dozens of square miles of water.

God, please give us wisdom. Please lead us to her.

Meagan was out there somewhere, frightened and alone with a psychotic killer. And all because she had done a good deed. She had seen someone who needed help, and had jumped right in and saved him.

And now she was in danger of losing her own life.

Realization shot through him, lightning fast and crystal clear. And he knew where Sally had taken her.

What better place to kill her than the exact location where the pilot had lost his life?

Meagan cruised down the main channel. The sky was awash with stars and an almost-full moon tipped the waves in silver. Its light would make her easier for Hunter and the others to spot. It would also make her easier for Sally to see, should she get the opportunity to try to escape.

She shifted on the seat, trying to relieve the tightness in her back. At this late hour, hers was the only boat in the vicinity. Sally sat in the front facing her, pistol at the ready. She kept glancing over her shoulder, tense and jittery. "Is this as fast as you can go?"

"It's only a four-horse motor." It wasn't wide open, but it was close. Meagan was holding back that final bit of power, giving Hunter and the others a few extra minutes to find her. It wouldn't be much, but minutes could count. They could mean the difference between life and death.

As soon as they had boarded the boat, Sally had ordered her to head for Seahorse Key. And it had been all Meagan could do to not run screaming into Darci's parents' house, which would have probably guaranteed them all a quick death.

Maybe Sally just wanted to see where her brother had died before she proceeded with her plans. But that wasn't likely. The most probable scenario was that Seahorse Key was the end of the trip, that Sally planned to kill her there, so the location and manner of death would resemble her brother's as closely as possible.

The terror Meagan had been trying to hold at bay for the past half hour circled through her, fraying the cords of control. She fought to stay calm. She had to keep her head. It was her only chance of surviving. And even then it would take a miracle.

And she wasn't a firm believer in miracles. Or any kind of divine intervention, for that matter. But Hunter was probably praying for her. In fact, she *knew* he was. Maybe God would listen to *him*.

Because He certainly wouldn't listen to *her*. After all, He had ignored the prayers of sweet, honest and generous Darci. Meagan sighed. She didn't stand a chance.

"How much farther?"

"I don't know, maybe another ten minutes." She pointed to a darker shape on the water a short distance ahead. "That's it there."

Sally's shoulders lifted, and her back straightened in anticipation. Meagan glanced behind her. There were no approaching bow lights in any direction. Maybe she was wrong. Maybe Hunter wouldn't figure it out and come after her. Maybe they were all searching Cedar Key for her, and no one would come.

She backed off the throttle, just slightly. But Sally noticed.

"Hey, keep going. Don't slow down."

A few minutes later, they approached the eastern

curve of Seahorse Key and Meagan eased the boat toward land. "This is it."

"No, I don't want to go ashore. I want you to take me to where the plane went down. I took a tour, and they said it happened right out there." She held up an index finger. "I know, because I asked."

Meagan changed course to head toward open water. Her heart pounded out an erratic rhythm, and her hand grew clammy against the throttle. Finally, she decreased speed until the motor was just idling.

"Is this the place?" Sally leaned forward, excitement rippling through her.

"This is it." Meagan's voice held a tone of finality.

Sally reached for the life jacket. There was only one. That was all Meagan could afford to replace at the time. If Sally planned to put it on, she would probably have to lay the gun down to fasten it.

Meagan waited in ready alertness. At the first opportunity, she would lunge for the woman, push her overboard and grab the gun. Her plan was risky. In fact, it was downright insane. But it was the only one she had.

But Sally didn't lay down the weapon. Instead, she struggled into the life jacket with one hand, then fastened the clasp, holding it steady with the heel of the hand grasping the gun.

Sally shook her head. "All those other ways I tried to kill you, you just wouldn't die. But this is so much more fitting. I feel as if I should thank you." Her eyes shone with a wild excitement. "Now get in the water."

Meagan froze, her thoughts fleeing in a dozen different directions.

No, she had to stay calm. The only weapon she had now was her words. She held up both hands.

"Sally, this isn't necessary. Your brother was a good

man. Is this what he would wish? Is this how he would want you to honor the life he lived?"

"I'm avenging his death. He would appreciate that."

"Are you sure? Did you ever know him to hurt anyone?" She was grasping at straws. She knew nothing about the pilot.

"None of that matters. All that matters is that you let him die." Sally aimed the gun at her chest. "Now stand up, or I'll shoot you right here in the boat and dump your body overboard."

The last spark of hope fled and darkness moved in, despair deeper than anything she had ever felt with Edmund. She was going to die. But if she had to choose between a bullet and drowning, she would choose the bullet.

Her thoughts turned heavenward. Was God really up there? Was He aware of what she was going through? Did He even care? Her gaze drifted past Sally. During the time they had idled, the bow had swung around, back toward the channel.

Anticipation surged through her, hope rekindled. Three boats were moving toward them. On the lead vessel, dual spotlights shone from about four or five feet above the water. The other boats were farther back, visible only because the bend of the channel separated them They were nothing but dark shapes on the waves, led by their red port bow lights.

Was the front one the fire rescue boat, and was Hunter in one of the others?

"Fine, have it your way." Sally pulled back the hammer and rested her index finger on the trigger.

Meagan's heart almost stopped. "Wait. I'll do what you say." And hope and pray that those approaching boats were for her. And that Sally wouldn't hear them over the soft putter of the four-horse.

The moment she was on her feet, Sally lunged toward her, knocking her off balance and over the side of the boat. Meagan hit the water with a splash.

Before she could recover, Sally jumped in, too, landing on top of her. Meagan's head snapped to the side, and several vertebrae cracked. Pain shot through her shoulder and neck, and water flowed into her nose. She broke the surface and tried to suck in air between coughing fits.

When she attempted to swim away, her foot met a firm thigh. Sally was right behind her. She had to get free. At least elude her long enough for help to arrive.

Two hands clamped down on her shoulders, forcing her under. She tried to break her captor's grip, but it only tightened, sending pain radiating down her arms. She fought with every bit of strength she possessed, twisting, kicking and clawing at the hands that held her. But Sally deflected each kick, and the fingernails digging into her hands and arms didn't seem to faze her. It was hopeless. With Sally in a life jacket and her wearing none, she didn't stand a chance.

God, help me. Let that be Hunter, and let him get here in time.

She had no idea if God would answer. Or if He had even heard. But those simple words prayed in desperation were the only chance she had left.

Her lungs began to burn, and the need for air soon eclipsed all other thought. She clamped her mouth shut, fighting against the urge to inhale. But the breath came anyway, involuntary and uncontrollable. Her throat closed, and spasms racked her body. Her diaphragm contracted, working to force the water from her lungs. But there was nothing to replace it except more water.

Terror gripped her, mixed with desperation. She had escaped Edmund, only to fall prey to a psychotic woman. She was moments from rescue, but was going to die.

Gradually, her spinning thoughts slowed and time seemed to hang suspended.

Then there was nothing.

EIGHT

Hunter sped down the channel, motor wide open. Blake was just ahead of him, their speeds matched. The Cedar Key Fire rescue boat had overtaken them both and was in the lead. *God, please let us get there in time.*

He tightened his grip on the throttle and offered up another desperate prayer, pleas for Meagan's protection. And prayers for his own state of mind.

Because ever since he'd barged into that bathroom and found it empty, he'd been half crazy with worry. If he didn't get a grip on his emotions, he wasn't going to be any good to Meagan or anyone else. He drew in a deep breath.

Maybe Blake was right. Maybe there *was* more between him and Meagan than he was willing to admit.

A vise clamped down on his heart. He didn't want to care for her in that way. He didn't want to care for *anyone* like that. His life was full and satisfying. And it was safe. At least in the way that mattered.

Career risks he could handle. Although Cedar Key was a low-crime town, there were dangers inherent to anyone who wore a uniform and carried a weapon. But he faced those dangers without flinching.

It was the other risks he wasn't willing to face—the

possibility that he might give his heart to someone and find he had fallen for a con. Or that he might allow his whole life to become wrapped up in another person, then have everything they had built snatched away in an instant.

He pushed the thoughts from his mind and squinted into the darkness. Seahorse Key was up ahead and to the right, a dark, stationary shape against the ever-moving surface of the sea. Beyond that... His pulse quickened and hope surged through him. Something sat a short distance off the key, a distinct shape, visible in the moonlight.

He strained to make it out. Yes, it was a boat, a small one, probably the size of Meagan's johnboat. There should be two people on board. But there were no shapes breaking the smooth profile. The boat appeared to be empty.

Which meant Meagan and Sally were already in the water.

His chest clenched. Knowing Meagan's past and her fear of drowning only made it worse. *God, help her to keep her cool. Help us to get there in time.* He pushed the throttle harder, but it was already at top speed.

As they drew closer, a small figure became visible, someone in a life jacket bobbing in the waves. He searched for a second person, his heart pounding. But there was only one. Sally Ferguson. Frantic prayers circled through his mind as he willed Meagan to surface.

The fire rescue boat was close now, its spotlights bathing the whole scene in sharp white light. Sally's head was tilted forward, her arms submerged. She didn't acknowledge their approach. She either didn't notice or was determined that nothing would stop her quest for revenge.

Despair showered down on him, hopelessness tinged with desperation. Meagan didn't even seem to be struggling. Maybe they were already too late.

The rescue boat slowed, and although Sally's head pivoted their direction, she didn't release her hold. Joe jumped into the water. Wade followed him moments later. Bobby and Gary remained on the boat. Bobby was in uniform, Gary wasn't, but both officers had their weapons drawn. Blake dropped to an idle, and Hunter did, too.

"Freeze!" It was Bobby who gave the order. "Hands in the air."

But Sally didn't move. When Joe grasped her arms, she struggled for several seconds, then tipped her head back and let out a bellow of rage-filled agony. Without warning, she swung a fist, catching Joe across the jaw.

Hunter stood, ready to take action. But he didn't need to. Bobby laid down his weapon and jumped in, removing the cuffs from his belt without pausing. He reached her within moments and soon had her restrained.

But Hunter's focus was on Wade. Joe had joined him, and they were lifting Meagan over the open back of the boat. Her eyes were closed, and she wasn't moving. She probably wasn't breathing, either. If only they could have gotten there three or four minutes sooner.

No, he wouldn't think like that. Joe and Wade were trained EMTs. They *would* revive her.

While they did CPR on Meagan, he tried to tune out Sally's screams of protest. Couldn't Bobby shut her up? He cast a glance that direction. Blake had pulled up alongside the rescue boat, and Gary had stepped aboard. Now they were loading a twisting and bucking Sally Ferguson aboard Blake's boat.

Hunter's eyes shifted back to Meagan, and he continued to send up prayers, alternating between pleading with God to save her and willing her to start breathing again. He longed to go to her, if for nothing more than to hold her hand, but he needed to stay back, to give Joe and Wade room to do their work.

In the background, his colleague's Southern drawl registered at the edge of his thoughts. Bobby was reading Sally her rights.

Finally, Meagan heaved, and water poured out onto the deck. Wade rolled her onto her side, and coughing spasms overtook her, expelling more water from her lungs. Then Joe covered her with a blanket.

Relief washed through Hunter, so intense he almost collapsed back onto the seat. *Thank You, thank You, thank You.* His prayers were answered. She was going to be all right. He shifted the motor into forward and pulled up alongside the rescue boat. Nothing was going to keep him away from her now.

He stepped aboard, and when Meagan sat up, Sally emitted a howl of rage. "No, it's not fair! She doesn't deserve to live! She killed him. She could have saved him, but didn't."

Bobby tried to calm her, but she wouldn't stop the flow of words.

"She saved the senator, because he was someone important. But she let my brother die."

Sally dropped her head and started to sob. "It's not fair. She's still alive, and he's gone. He's all I had. I loved him. And I know he loved me. For the first time, I was happy."

For the first time? What was she talking about? She had lived with her brother for the past ten years.

She sobbed even harder. "He was going to take me away. He promised. And she ruined it."

Take her away? On a trip? She was making less and less sense.

She drew in some jagged breaths and continued. "I always had a hard time finding someone. And finally Jarrod came along."

Jarrod? Who was Jarrod? Her brother's name was Bruce.

"She could have had any guy she wanted. But she had to go after Jarrod. She took him away from me."

Sally suddenly grew calm. Hunter watched the wildness flee her eyes, and though she turned toward him and the others aboard the rescue boat, her gaze didn't really settle there. Her focus seemed to be somewhere far beyond them. Or in the distant past.

When she continued, her tone was flat, without emotion. "I can't have him, but she can't, either."

Hunter's eyes widened as realization stuck him. This was no longer about the pilot. Or even about Meagan. It was about the incident when she was sixteen years old. The fight over a guy. And her friend's suspicious death.

Bobby leaned toward her, his voice low. "Why can't she have him?"

Hunter watched her slowly shift her gaze. When she spoke, her words, and the coldness behind them, sent a chill all the way to his core.

"Because I killed her."

Hunter dropped to his knees next to Meagan and took her hands in his. Her grip was surprisingly strong. She would need to go to the hospital to be checked out, and he would follow her there. Then, if she would let him, he would sleep on her couch. He didn't want her to be alone when she woke up screaming from a nightmare, as he was sure she would.

Blake motioned toward the channel. "I'll take these guys back, and they can get her booked in."

Meagan sat up straighter. "Wait. Check my boat. Sally had a gun."

Blake eased up to it, and Bobby reached in with a cloth and retrieved a 9 mm with a suppressor. "This baby could have done some damage, and nobody would have known." He eased back into his seat. "So how are we getting Meagan's boat back?"

Hunter held up a hand. "I'll tow it." Once he returned it to the beach at the Tucker place, he would take care of his own boat, then head for the hospital.

As Blake sped away with his three passengers, Wade knelt next to Meagan. "We need to take you to the ER. You've been through quite an ordeal and should be checked out."

Meagan's hand tightened on his, as if it was her life-line to safety. "No." She shook her head. "I want to stay with Hunter."

Both Wade and Joe looked at him with raised brows, and one corner of Wade's mouth cocked up. No, it wasn't like that, regardless of the emotion exploding in his heart at the moment. It was just that Meagan knew him better than any of the others. She had reached a level of comfort with him, maybe even trusted him.

Wade again grew serious. "Meagan, you need to be treated. You've got water in your lungs."

"No, I coughed it up. I'm breathing fine."

"You're breathing fine now, but even a little bit of fluid could be dangerous."

She shook her head, jaw set. Her stubbornness could be exasperating. Tonight it was understandable. After all she had been through, spending several hours in a hospital emergency room was probably the last thing she felt like doing. But he wasn't willing to take chances with her life.

"Will you go if I take you and stay with you?"

Several moments passed while she pondered his question. Finally she nodded.

After he helped her onto his boat, she settled into the seat opposite his and drew in a shaky breath. "It's all over."

"Yes, it is. You're safe now."

He accelerated, but set the throttle at about half the speed he had used coming out. If she wanted to talk, he wouldn't make her shout over the roar of the motor.

"How did you know where to find me?"

He eased the throttle back further. Her voice was soft. He had heard her, but just barely. "I talked to a couple who saw you headed down Third toward the water."

She nodded, still staring straight ahead. "I remember them. I thought about trying to signal them, to let them know I needed help. But Sally said if I did, she'd kill them." Meagan turned to look at him. "I couldn't risk anyone else's life to save my own."

He reached across and patted her shoulder. "You did good."

She sighed and pulled the blanket more tightly around her. "The pilot drowned."

A hollow emptiness spread through him. Obviously, Sally had gotten ahold of the autopsy report and had told Meagan what it said.

"I'm sorry."

He longed to reach out to her, to offer comfort. But there was nothing he could say that would erase what she now knew. Although he didn't take his eyes off the course ahead, he could feel her watching him.

"You knew, didn't you?"

He couldn't lie. It would be so much easier if he could.

"You knew and didn't tell me."

"I'm sorry. I knew how much it would upset you."

"So instead of finding it out from you, I learned it from her." Meagan's anger came through in her tone, infusing her voice with strength that hadn't been there moments earlier.

"Meagan, please don't be angry with me. I was trying to protect you."

"It's not your place to protect me." She crossed her arms inside the blanket and twisted in the seat so she was angled away from him.

He backed off the throttle until the engine was just idling. "I saw how much it bothered you that you weren't able to get the pilot out of the plane. That was when you thought he was already dead. When I found out that he was alive when the plane sank, I knew that would cause you even more grief. Unnecessary grief. I didn't want to hurt you."

He reached up to touch the side of her face, and she flinched, almost imperceptibly. He dropped his hand. "You don't need to be afraid of me, Meagan. I would never hurt you." He lifted his hand again and traced the line of her jaw with one finger, his touch feather-light. "Not all men are abusive. In fact, most men aren't. There's someone out there who is going to appreciate you for all that you are—your talent, your spunk, your gentleness, your care for others. He's going to show you what it's like to feel loved and cared for and cherished above all else."

Her eyes fluttered closed, and she rested her cheek against the palm of his hand. She looked secure. At peace. Two things she hadn't experienced much in recent months, probably in over a year.

And she was beautiful.

"Show me." Her words came out in the softest whisper.

His pulse rate tripled, and his stomach went into a free fall.

Show me. Did she know what she was asking? That if he showed her what it was like to feel loved and cared for and cherished, he couldn't do it without putting his heart and soul into it? That doing so would fan to life embers he had let die years ago? That the very thought filled him with his own brand of fear?

A droplet of water fell from her bangs and caught in her lashes before breaking loose to run down her cheek. It stopped when it reached her mouth. His thumb traced its path, lingering on her lips. The silence of the night wrapped around them, and moonlight bathed them in its silvery glow.

Something stirred within him, a long-suppressed force awakening. Her eyes drifted open, and her gaze locked with his. There was no tension there, no fear. Her eyes held only longing, mirroring his own.

He slid from his seat to kneel next to her, then leaned toward her, drawn by invisible cords. But she didn't pull away. Instead, her eyes closed and her lips parted, inviting him closer still.

He kissed her, the brush of his lips as soft as his other touch had been. But there was nothing gentle about the effect she had on him. Fire coursed all the way to his toes, and he fought the urge to crush her to him.

Despite the firestorm of emotion swirling through him, he held back. Beneath the strength and resourcefulness that she showed to the world was a fragility that spoke to everything masculine in him. Tenderness shot through him, followed by determination. He would show her that other men weren't like Edmund and her father. He would treat her with gentleness and care and respect.

And she would know what it felt like to be loved.

The thought was like a dash of cold water thrown into his face. He backed away and returned to his seat. He was offering her something that wasn't his to give, making promises he would never be able to keep.

The boat moved with a gentle rocking motion, mocking the turmoil within him.

"I'm sorry."

"Sorry for what? That you kissed me?" Her eyes held sadness. And loss. As if she had touched something wonderful for the briefest moment before it slipped through her hands.

Or maybe that was what he felt.

She frowned over at him. "Why do you do it? Why do you pour yourself into work and church and volunteer activities, to the exclusion of relationships?"

"I don't exclude relationships. I have a lot of close friendships."

"During the four years you've lived on Cedar Key, no one has known you to have a girlfriend or even go on a date. And it's not because no one is interested. Half the town's female population would kill for a chance to be with the elusive Hunter Kingston."

"I think someone's doing a lot of exaggerating." He laughed, but it sounded hollow, even to his own ears.

"What happened? Why are you afraid?"

"I'm not afraid." The argument flowed out with no forethought.

Meagan untangled her arm from the blanket and put a hand on his shoulder. "Tell me. What happened to you? Did someone leave you?"

He drew in a deep breath, preparing to speak the sentence that he always avoided vocalizing aloud. In fact, he tried to avoid thinking about it, too. "She was killed by a drunk driver three weeks before our wedding."

"I'm so sorry." Meagan dropped her arm.

Four years ago, he had vowed that he would never open himself up to that kind of pain again. He had never been willing to break that vow.

Until now.

What he was feeling was a mistake. He didn't want to fall in love again. And he didn't want to fall in love with Meagan. She had deceived everyone on Cedar Key. It wasn't that he didn't understand, because he did. He could justify everything she had done. But she was a good liar. Too good. Like his brother. How would he ever be able to fully trust her?

He eased the throttle forward. He needed to get a grip on his emotions. But that would take keeping his distance from Meagan.

The problem was, he didn't want to keep his distance. In fact, he wanted to wrap her in his arms and kiss her until all the raw places in his heart healed over.

And every bad experience she had ever had was nothing but a distant memory.

The sun shone from high in a cloudless sky, its heat tempered by the cool breeze blowing off the Gulf. Meagan drew in a cleansing breath and let it out slowly. Two days had passed since Sally's capture. Two whole days of living without fear. Two days of freedom.

She smiled over at Blake's wife, Allison. Blake had left them in search of something to drink. They currently stood in the park, enjoying the sunshine and mild temperatures, along with dozens of…pirates. On the beach, a bunch of them had formed two rows and squared off.

Musket fire boomed, and smoke rose. Between them, two pirates lay dead next to a treasure chest.

But it was all in good fun. It was the weekend of the annual Cedar Key Pirate Invasion. The day had started with pirates invading the city park, then sauntering through the streets in full garb, singing pirate songs. Now was the epic Battle for Cedar Key, wherein Jean Lafitte's men tried to remove his treasure from the island, while pirates from all over tried to take it. The Spanish Garrison was there to keep the peace.

"Hey, ladies."

Meagan turned to see Hunter approach, handsome as always in his police uniform. He smiled, and her heart gave an answering flutter.

She had spent Thursday night and part of yesterday in the hospital. Then Hunter had brought her home. He had offered to sleep on her couch so she wouldn't have to be alone, at least that first night, but she had declined the offer. Knowing he was lying twenty feet away would have kept her awake until the wee hours of the morning.

Especially after that kiss. No one had ever kissed her like that. Or made her feel the way Hunter had. She kept reminding herself that it didn't mean anything. She had, in so many words, asked him to kiss her. She had wanted him to show her what it was like to feel loved and cherished.

And he had. So well that she didn't want it to end. But it wasn't real. At least it wasn't personal. That was just the way Hunter was—gentle, caring, concerned for others.

And as long as he kept his heart closed, he wouldn't *let* it be real. With anyone. But that didn't stop her pulse from skipping a beat every time he approached, or keep her from longing for what she could never have.

She shook off the thoughts and returned Hunter's smile. "Hey, yourself."

"I thought you were supposed to be at the store today."

"I was, but Darci gave me the day off. She didn't want me to miss the activities."

Meagan had taken yesterday off, too. It had been so late when she got in Thursday night, and when Darci heard what had happened, she was adamant—Meagan needed time for some rest and relaxation. Darci promised she could make up the hours next week.

Blake returned with three bottles of water. After some casual conversation, Hunter turned to go back to his duties, most of which involved roaming the crowds and making sure the only thieving and rabble-rousing going on were part of the planned activities. Hunter's shift would end at six. Then he would meet Blake and Allison and Meagan for dinner. If it weren't for the fact that Darci and Jayden would be joining them, it would feel a lot like a double date. Except Hunter didn't date.

As Meagan watched him walk away, a sigh escaped her mouth. She had come to Cedar Key determined that no man would ever again charm his way into her life. But Hunter had a way of blowing holes through barricades without even trying.

"Don't give up on him."

Blake's words cut across her thoughts. "What?"

"Don't give up on him. Right now, he doesn't know what he wants. But I'm working on him."

Was she that obvious? "He might not appreciate you playing matchmaker."

"I'm just returning the favor." Blake put his arm around his wife and pulled her close. "He put *us* together."

"Well," Allison interjected, "not exactly put us together. More like knocked some sense into *him* when he was going to leave Cedar Key and go back to Texas."

Meagan laughed. "That's a story I want to hear sometime." She loved happy endings. They just always seemed to belong to someone else.

As the sun sank low, the three of them made their way down Dock Street to the Seabreeze. When Hunter, Darci and Jayden arrived, they had just been seated.

Allison smiled up at the newcomers. "Perfect timing. Are you hungry?"

"Hungry and thankful to get off my feet for an hour or so." Hunter sank into one of the two empty chairs. The third was a high chair.

By the time their meals arrived, the final remnants of daylight were fading to dusk. Pirates still roamed the streets, along with residents and visitors who had just come to observe. The table where Meagan and her friends were sitting was on the side. Large windows offered an unbroken view of the park. This weekend, it was home to an authentic pirate encampment, as well as Thieves Row, a dozen or so pirate-themed vendors.

Two men moved down the sidewalk toward her, navigating the curve where A Street became Dock. They were dressed in full pirate garb, their tricorne hats casting their faces in shadow. One was tall and slender, the other shorter and stocky.

Meagan tensed, unease trickling through her. Based on their sizes, they could be Edmund and Lou. Of course, they could also be any number of other men on Cedar Key that day. She silently scolded herself. If she was going to have any semblance of a happy life, she was going to have to stop looking for the devil under every rock.

Then the taller pirate tipped back his head, and for a

brief moment, his eyes locked with hers. Actually, it was just one eye—the other was covered with a black patch.

She let out a gasp. All conversation at the table stopped, and every head except Jayden's turned to her.

Meagan tightened her hand around her fork. "I think I just saw Edmund." She had nothing to hide. Darci knew her past. So did Blake. Allison likely didn't, but Blake could explain later.

Allison's eyes widened. "Are you sure?"

Okay, so she knew, too. Meagan didn't mind. Allison had experienced her own terror.

"I—I think so." The eye contact had been brief, not more than a second or two. But he had looked right at her. And projected hatred—cold and lethal.

Or maybe it was her imagination. Maybe it wasn't Edmund at all.

"It looked just like him. And he was with someone Lou's size. But I could be wrong. The lighting isn't good."

She tried to push the concerns from her mind, determined to enjoy her dinner. But later, as people gathered in front of the Seabreeze and formed a large circle to watch the fire performers, she found herself scanning the faces of the crowd. Then the music started, and within moments, she was mesmerized.

Flames lit up the darkness as the dancers stepped and turned and twisted to a rock beat. One performer held what looked like a long baton, lit at both ends. He twirled it in front, overhead and behind his back, at times so quickly that there almost seemed to be an unbroken circle of fire. A female performer had a flame trailing from each arm. She dropped to her knees, then eased herself backward until she was lying faceup, with the flames dipping and twirling over her body.

As the first song ended and the second one began, Meagan cast a glance at Hunter. She started to return her attention to the performers, but one of the observers caught her gaze and held it. It was the tall pirate. The flickering light cast dancing shadows across his face, but she had no doubt he was watching her.

She grasped Hunter's forearm and held it in a vise-like grip. "There he is."

"Where?"

She pointed almost straight across the circle. "Over there, in the tricorne hat and eye patch."

Hunter looked at her askance. "You just described several dozen people."

The crowd shifted, and the tall pirate fell back. Maybe it wasn't Edmund. But maybe it was. Either way, she had to know.

She grabbed Hunter's hand and pulled him around the back of the circle. Then she stood on her tiptoes, searching.

Just as she caught a glimpse of him, a heavyset man moved to the side and blocked her view. By the time she was able to slip around him, she had lost the tall pirate.

At the end of Dock Street, she broke from the crowd and looked up A Street toward the park. There they were. The pair she had seen from the window of the Seabreeze.

She charged off in that direction, Hunter right on her heels. They caught up to the two men between the boat ramp and the park.

"Hey, you. Stop." Hunter's voice held undeniable authority. He still wore the uniform to back it up.

The men spun around. Neither had an eye patch and neither was Edmund or Lou. They had followed the wrong men.

Or maybe they hadn't. Maybe the men she'd seen

from the Seabreeze were just ordinary people, in Cedar Key for a good time.

Hunter looked at her, clearly waiting for direction.

She offered the men a weak smile. "I'm sorry. We mistook you for someone else."

Hunter held up a hand. "Sorry to bother you. Go about your evening."

She dropped her gaze to the sidewalk, embarrassment washing over her. "I'm sorry. I just led you on a wild-goose chase."

Hunter hooked a finger under her chin and gently tilted her face upward until she was looking at him.

"Don't ever apologize for letting me know you feel threatened. And don't ever feel like you can't come to me with any concerns. I don't care how small they seem."

He stared down at her, his gaze tender. It was the same gentleness she had felt in his kiss. And longed to experience again, but refused to ask.

She cleared her throat and shifted her weight. "Thanks. I'll probably be doing a lot of that."

Chances were good that she was worrying for nothing, that Edmund never saw the report about the plane crash. A month and a half had passed. There was the possibility that Lou had visited Nature's Landing, but other than that, Edmund hadn't attempted to come after her.

He was patient, though—cold and calculating. And he was careful. He wouldn't risk getting caught.

The pirate festival offered the perfect opportunity. What better time to come looking for her than during an event that drew hundreds of people?

An event one could attend in costume and slip in and out of the crowd undetected.

Then strike when least expected.

NINE

The final strains of guitar and keyboard filtered through the sanctuary, then faded to silence. Meagan stood with her hands resting on the pew in front of her, Hunter on one side and Blake on the other.

She had finally done it. Although both Hunter and Darci had invited her several times, she had always managed to come up with an excuse not to attend church with them. Then last night, after the pirate festival, Allison had hit her up. Meagan must have been feeling especially vulnerable, because before she knew what she was doing, she had agreed to come.

Maybe it was the months of isolation—first imposed by Edmund, then the prison she had erected around herself to keep others from finding out her secret. If so, that was only part of it.

Last night Wade and Sydney had joined them, and they had all gone over to Allison and Blake's for cake and ice cream. And as Meagan sat listening to the laughter and the teasing and the storytelling, a hollow emptiness had started deep inside, a need to belong.

These people weren't just friends. They were family. And although most of them knew her background, they accepted her as one of them.

Meagan took a seat with the other worshippers while
Allison and Darci made their way off the platform. They
had both sung with the praise team, and their job was
apparently finished, at least for the time being. Allison
circled around to sit next to Blake, and Darci chose a
seat on the other side of Hunter. She reached across him
to squeeze Meagan's hand, her face radiant.

Meagan smiled over at her. Looking at Darci, one
would think her life was all sunshine and happiness.
But Meagan knew better. Darci had found the secret
to having joy *in spite of* what was going on around her.
All the people who had sat in Allison's living room last
night had discovered it, too. And the common denomi-
nator was their faith.

So aside from the need for friendship, there was one
other thing that had lured her out of the house on a Sunday morning. She was on a quest. For what, she wasn't
sure. But something told her whatever it was that her
new friends seemed to possess, it was probably offered
at the small white church on the corner.

When the service was over, she made her way down
the aisle toward the back, while the worship team per-
formed "Friend of God." That had been the topic of the
pastor's sermon, one she had found intriguing.

Sometimes she thought of God as the Creator, having spoken everything into being, then turned it loose.
Other times she thought of Him as the Judge, ready to
zap people with lightning bolts if they got too out of line.
Usually she didn't think of Him at all.

But *Friend*? That was a new concept. Maybe that
was what Hunter was referring to when he said that
while God didn't always keep His people from trouble,
he walked with them *through* it. That didn't take away
from Him being Creator and Judge and probably a dozen

other titles. But thinking of Him as Friend had appeal. Maybe because she had been without one for too long.

Once they stepped into the sunshine, Hunter led her to his truck. He had insisted on picking her up, even though Sydney and Wade would be driving right past her house.

"What are you doing for lunch?"

"Warming up leftover enchiladas." She grinned at him. "That's the problem with living alone. You'd better like whatever you cook, because you're going to be eating on it for the next three days."

"Tell me about it." He unlocked the passenger door and helped her in.

"If you like Mexican, you're welcome to join me."

"Since I've got to be at the station in an hour, I think I'll take you up on that."

A few minutes later, Hunter waited on her porch while she inserted her key into the lock. She tensed, a sense of uneasiness sliding through her. It wasn't that long ago that they had been in this exact location and Hunter had been shot with an arrow.

But Sally was no longer a threat. And taking potshots from across the street wasn't Edmund's style. She shook off the uneasiness and led Hunter inside. He helped her set the table, and once she had warmed the enchiladas, she took a seat opposite him.

Conversation started out light, but soon creases appeared between Hunter's brows. "Are you staying inside the rest of the day?"

"I'm planning to. I might work on some painting. Or I might be lazy and read this afternoon. I picked up two paperbacks at a garage sale and haven't gotten to them yet."

He nodded. "I'm going to patrol past here regularly. Blake and Bobby are going to be driving by, too. And if you see anything suspicious, you know to call." The creases between his brows deepened, and his eyes darkened with concern. "I'm a little uneasy with the idea that Edmund might have been in Cedar Key yesterday."

"Yeah. Me, too." She tried to force a smile. "But maybe it was just someone who looked like him. They say everyone has a twin somewhere in the world." She cut off a bite and picked it up with her fork, but didn't put it in her mouth. "Actually, Edmund really does have a twin. In Italy. They were born Eduardo and Edmondo. But Edmondo changed his name to Edmund when he came to America."

Hunter's expression grew thoughtful. "Are they identical twins?"

"Yeah. I've never met Eduardo, but I've seen pictures. And you can't tell them apart." They had the same angled features, the same jet-black hair, the same dark charm. Even the same cruelness in their eyes.

"Eduardo may have provided Edmund with his alibi."

Her eyes widened. "I hadn't thought of that."

"It would be interesting to see if Eduardo took a flight from Italy to California just before Charlie's death."

"Interesting, but still not enough to convict Edmund of murder. I'm not willing to go up against him unless it's an open-and-shut case." And she would have her doubts, even then. "I was so afraid he was going to figure out what I was doing before I got a chance to make my escape. He and Lou were both watching me so closely, I was lucky I got out of there."

Or maybe it wasn't luck. Maybe God had had a hand in it. That was what Hunter believed.

"How did you manage to get fake IDs made?"

"I found a website where you can order them. I took a picture of myself, edited it with Photoshop to give myself short, dark hair, and emailed it to them. But I knew I couldn't just have the IDs sent in an envelope addressed to me. Lou always inspected my mail before handing it over."

Hunter laid down his fork, but didn't lean back in the chair, even though he had finished eating. "So what did you do?"

"I paid them an extra hundred dollars to purchase and send me three tubes of paint, and address the box from American Artist Supplies. I had them put the fake Social Security card and Florida driver's license in a blank envelope under the paint. I figured if Edmund or Lou checked the box and found the envelope, I'd just say it apparently belonged to an employee at the store, and I'd call and straighten it out."

"Wow, you thought of everything." Respect shone in Hunter's eyes. "That was brilliant."

She shrugged, suddenly feeling shy. "It's amazing what you can come up with when your life is at stake. The only trail I couldn't cover was the credit card I used to pay for all that. But I hadn't used the card in over a year." She hadn't needed to. Edmund had insisted on paying for everything. "The credit card company still had my old PO box and no forwarding address. So I figured I was pretty safe."

Hunter pushed back his chair and stood, but there was reluctance in the motion. "If I'm going to make it to work on time, I'd better get going."

She walked him to the door, but instead of stepping over the threshold, he turned to face her. "Are you going to be okay alone?"

"I'll be fine. If not, I've got my phone. You go on."

He hesitated a moment longer. Concern had crept back into his eyes. He lifted a hand and cupped her jaw with his palm. The worry was still obvious on his face, along with something else—indecision. Was it possible Hunter was struggling with the same feelings for her that she was for him? Her stomach rolled over at the thought. But what difference would it make? As long as he kept his heart guarded, it didn't matter what he felt; he would never act on it.

He let his hand fall. "Stay inside…please."

She gave him an uneasy smile. "You won't get any argument from me."

After watching him walk to his truck, she closed and locked the door, then leaned against it with a sigh. Not only was he more handsome than any man had a right to be, but he was honest and gentle and caring and self-less and…his good qualities were too many to name. No wonder so many of the single women in Cedar Key had fantasies of someday winning Hunter's heart.

Meagan pushed herself away from the door and headed toward her desk. The Visqueen she had used to protect its surface Friday afternoon was still there, her latest project lying on top. She frowned down at her work. The reading she had mentioned earlier sounded really good. Immersing herself in someone else's life for a few hours held a lot of appeal.

She opened the desk drawer and pulled out one of the paperback books, then rested her leg against the drawer, ready to push it closed. Beneath the other paperback was the old book of poetry. For almost four months it had lain there untouched. She hadn't been able to bring herself to read it. It reminded her too much of California, her life with Edmund, everything she had left behind.

But now it seemed to call to her. Maybe it was time to move on. She was a survivor. She had survived not only Edmund, but Sally, too. She had found new friends, good friends, and begun a search for meaning in her life. It was time to come to terms with all that had happened in the past and put it behind her.

She reached into the drawer and pulled out the old book. As she settled onto the couch, a wonderful sense of contentment filled her. Nothing had changed. She was still an unknown artist working part time in a small gift shop to try to make ends meet. She was still cut off from her family, filled with longing to see them again. But now her focus was on what she had gained instead of what she had lost. And the future looked much brighter because of it.

She let the book fall open to a random page one third of the way through, and her eyes dipped to the title, "How Did You Die?" by Edmund Vance Cooke. Maybe the page wasn't so random. The poem was a favorite of both hers and Charlie's, read and reread so many times the volume naturally fell open there. The theme was facing trouble with strength and character, and during her darkest moments with Edmund, she had returned to it again and again for encouragement to keep going and not give up. And Charlie apparently had, too.

At the time, they both had "trouble a ton." Charlie had brought a lot of his on himself. But he didn't deserve to die. Edmund had snuffed out the life of a creative, kind-hearted man, and had gotten away with it.

Meagan's heart twisted at the thought. Other than Edmund and possibly Lou, she was the only person alive who knew the truth. But there was nothing she could do about it. Even if she had the courage to go up against Edmund, she didn't have the power, strength or financial resources. No one did.

She turned the page and began to read the next poem, determined to banish Edmund from her thoughts. Someday she would be able to pick up the book and just enjoy it for the beautiful, thought-provoking words, and not be reminded of its link to California and Edmund and a yearlong ordeal that she hadn't been sure she would survive.

That would have been Charlie's wish, that the book would provide her many hours of enjoyment. He had known that what he was attempting was risky, that he might not leave Edmund's estate alive. So he had left the book in the atrium where she would be the one to find it.

She read several more poems, skipping large sections, choosing pages at random. Then she flipped to the back. It had been a library book at one time. The sleeve that had held the card was still there, although the card had been removed long ago.

Meagan frowned. There was a small bulge in the center of the pouch. She reached in with two fingers and pulled out something hard and flat. A memory card. Did it belong to Charlie?

Confusion warred with anticipation. It had to have been his. No one else ever handled the book besides the two of them. Did the card just hold ordinary pictures, and the pouch happened to be a convenient place to tuck it at the time?

Or was it what he'd claimed to have found, the evidence that would put Edmund away? Had Charlie put it in there the night he was killed, hoping she would find it if his plan went awry?

Meagan swung her feet down from the coffee table and headed to her room. She didn't have a computer, but she had a camera. Hopefully, the card would fit. It looked compatible.

Within moments, she had pulled her camera from its bag, removed the old card and inserted the new one.

After a few clicks, a picture filled the screen. A tree stood against a blue sky, although with the small size of the display, she couldn't tell what kind.

She advanced to the next frame. It was another landscape photo, grass dotted with wildflowers, greenery in the background. The next several pictures were more of the same.

Her heart fell. The card just contained samples of his work. She clicked through the rest of the pictures, not giving them much more than a cursory glance. Then she got to one that was different and had to back up when she moved past it.

The photo seemed to have been shot at more of a downward angle. There was no sky visible in the upper one third, as with the others. Wildflowers filled the entire frame, except for a darkened area at the bottom. Was it the edge of a hole?

A chill swept through her, and the fine hairs on her neck stood on end. She advanced to the next picture. The darkened area on the previous slide was definitely a hole. This shot was taken from above, looking down.

Something was there, in the dirt—fabric and a stick or rod of some type, and… Ice pumped slowly through her veins and lodged in her core. She set down the camera and picked up her phone. Hunter answered on the second ring.

She got right to the point. "Come quick. And bring your laptop. I've found something you need to see."

She couldn't be sure. The display was too small. And the lighting in the pictures wasn't good. They seemed to have been taken late in the day, because there was a lot of shadow.

But something about the last photo didn't look right. Something had been buried, and someone had dug it up. And even though she couldn't tell with certainty, if she had to make a guess, she would say she was looking at a body.

Hunter resisted the urge to use the siren and lights and instead cruised down Fifth Street at, or close to, the speed limit. Meagan hadn't given him any details, but the anticipation in her voice was unmistakable. She had found something important. And it had apparently shown up in the hour since he'd left.

He eased to a stop in her driveway and jumped from the car, laptop in hand. The door swung inward before he even stepped onto the porch, and she appeared in the opening holding a camera.

As soon as he was inside, she removed the card and handed it to him. "Check this out."

He slid it into the slot in the front of his laptop, and once he had positioned himself on the couch, she sat next to him.

"Where did you get this?"

"I have a book of poems that I got from Charlie. It's an old library book. The memory card was in the pocket in the back."

A window popped up on the screen. He chose the top folder and clicked on the first picture. Some kind of tree seemed to be the focal point. Other greenery filled the distant background. Except for a band of blue sky at the top, a multicolored blanket of wildflowers filled the rest of the space. After studying the screen for several moments, he looked at Meagan. "This is it?"

"Keep going."

The next picture was almost identical to the first, except the tree was missing. He advanced to the next and the next, which were more of the same. But the angle of the greenery in the distance was different, as if the photographer had pivoted slightly prior to each shot.

Hunter frowned. Surely she didn't call him over to look at landscaping ideas. "Very pretty, but I don't see the significance."

"I think they're hints. Landmarks."

"For what?"

"Keep scrolling and you'll see."

As he clicked through the photos, the background changed gradually, varying in the types of plants, but the foreground remained constant. The photographer had never left his post in the center of the field.

"I'm assuming at some point this gets more interesting."

"Oh, it gets a lot more interesting."

After two more photos, he stopped. This one was different. The camera was angled downward. Except for the edge of a hole at the bottom of the screen and the trunk of a tree at the top, the shot consisted entirely of wildflowers.

He pointed. "I wonder if that's the same tree that's in the first picture."

"It is. A black walnut."

He glanced at her again. "You can tell that from just looking at the trunk?"

"No. I know this field. It's on Edmund's estate. And that's the only tree in it."

"Could you direct someone to this location? Without going there yourself, I mean."

"I could."

He clicked to the next picture, and Meagan flinched. He understood why. She had probably already viewed it on her camera. But two by three inches didn't do it justice.

Eight by fourteen did.

The shot was taken directly into the hole. In the bottom was a body. Dirt-covered clothing draped little more than a skeleton. A shaft protruded from the chest, the remains of an arrow. Its point was still buried in the rib cage, its other end broken off. Whoever had dumped the body into the hole hadn't bothered to throw a cloth over the face. But fortunately, Charlie hadn't fully uncovered it. The teeth and jaw were visible, but the rest of the skull was hidden from view.

"Edmund's ex-fiancée?"

Meagan swallowed hard. "I would say so."

"Do you think Charlie knew about it all along, or do you think he stumbled on it unknowingly?"

"I think he stumbled on it. He knew I loved the gardens. I would get my inspiration out there and do my sketching. There and the atrium. Then I would go into my studio and paint. Charlie was always adding things to make me happy. He had a gambling problem, but I have to say, he had a good heart."

She drew in a shaky breath. "About a month before he was killed, he said he was going to do something special for my birthday. He told me to stay out of the field, that he wanted it to be a surprise. I don't know what he had in mind, but apparently, when he started digging, he found her."

"Did you ever go out there after he died?"

"Not for about a month."

"Was anything different when you went?"

Meagan shook her head. "It didn't look like he had really done anything. But there was one spot where the grass and wildflowers were thinner and shorter. I didn't think anything of it at the time. I just figured that Charlie had left it dug up, and someone else had come along and tried to fill the wildflowers back in."

"The million-dollar question is whether Edmund was smart enough to move the body."

"He may have not seen the need. I mean, the only two people in the world who knew his secret were Charlie and I'm guessing Lou, since Edmund might have used his help to dispose of the body. As long as he got rid of Charlie, he was safe. Lou wasn't likely to talk, or he would be implicating himself along with Edmund."

Hunter clicked forward to see if there were any more pictures. There were—two more, the second probably taken in case the first didn't turn out, and a third also taken for backup before he'd once again covered the hole.

Meagan drew in a deep breath and let it out slowly. "So where do we go from here?"

"I'll talk to Chief Sandlin, and we'll get in touch with California. We'll get them the pictures." Now they made sense—all the shots, the seemingly meaningless repetition. Charlie was trying to show them the exact location of what he had found.

"Charlie wasn't educated, but I knew he was smart. Besides liking good poetry, he was great at figuring things out. All those shots he took make up a panoramic photo. Someone who really knew what they were doing could analyze each of the photos and pinpoint the exact location of that hole."

Hunter made several clicks, then closed the computer. "I saved the photos to my hard drive, just in case."

"Good idea. I'd hate to lose that card."

"I'll hang on to it and give it to Chief Sandlin. He'll turn it over to the authorities in California, along with Charlie's blackmail letter."

"And," she added, "the information about his brother.

He's got a pretty watertight alibi as it stands. But if we can prove Eduardo flew over here and flew back a few days later, that will cast doubt on it."

Meagan stood and rounded the coffee table. Excitement radiated from her as she shifted her weight from one foot to the other, coming up on her toes, then back down again. She was nearly dancing. "It's almost over."

Hunter laid down his laptop and went to stand in front of her. He wanted to caution her that it wasn't over until it was over, to not let down her guard. But her enthusiasm was infectious. Before he realized what he was doing, he'd wrapped her in a hug, then lifted her and spun her around. When he put her back down, instead of releasing her, he kept her locked in his embrace.

She looped her arms around his neck and smiled up at him. "Edmund will be going to jail for a long time. After a year and a half of bondage, I'll finally be free." Her eyes twinkled, and her face glowed with happiness. All the underlying tension that had infused her features since the moment he had met her seemed to have vanished. This was the real Meagan, the pre-Edmund Meagan. And he liked what he saw.

Without warning, she rose to her tiptoes and pressed her mouth to his. It wasn't like the kiss on his boat. It was spontaneous and lighthearted and joyous.

And much too brief.

An unexpected longing surged through him. What would she do if he kissed her—*really* kissed her—and poured everything he felt into it? Not because she had asked him to, but because it was what he had wanted to do for the past three days?

Before he could contemplate further, she slid from his arms and stepped back to take his hands in hers. She was still smiling, but it was tempered with caution.

"Don't worry. I know I'm not actually safe until Edmund is captured, so I'll be careful."

He squeezed her hands, trying to shake off the effects of her nearness. "Good. And we'll all keep our eyes open, too. If anything, we'll step up security, because if he gets wind of what you found, it could put you in even more danger."

Worry tightened his gut. There was a lot that could go wrong. For this to work, the police needed to get in and out without Edmund being tipped off. And they needed to find a body. Lastly, they needed something to blow his alibi.

Hopefully, every piece of the puzzle would fall into place.

Edmund needed to be brought to justice.

Because Meagan gaining her freedom depended on Edmund losing his.

A crisp breeze blew out of the north, the first sign of fall. After a long, hot summer, the cool morning air was refreshing.

Meagan pedaled slowly down D Street on Darci's bike. It was a loaner, but Darci had insisted she keep it indefinitely. It felt good to be on a bicycle again, somewhat independent, even though someone would always have to accompany her. This time it was Sydney, jogging next to her, holding Chandler's leash. The little dachshund seemed to have an endless supply of energy and had no problem keeping up.

After a conversation with Sydney last night, Meagan had timed a trip to The Market to coincide with Chandler's morning walk. Except today it was a run, which Chandler seemed to enjoy more, anyway. And somewhere nearby was likely a detective. Or two. Hunter still insisted that she not go anywhere alone. And for the time being, she was happy to comply.

She eased to a stop, and after waiting for traffic to clear, turned onto Fifth. Several big green trash cans dotted each side of the street. Monday was garbage collection day. Three yards down, the top of one of the containers was sticking up, an orange object keeping it from closing all the way.

Meagan drew closer, then squeezed the brakes. The orange object looked like a life jacket. She lifted the lid and pulled it out. It was adult-sized and, except for being a little faded, was in perfect condition.

"I'm taking this to my boat. You probably heard what happened to mine."

"Wade told me." Sydney shook her head. "Thank the Lord she's not a threat anymore."

Wade told her. Meagan sighed. It seemed everyone in Cedar Key knew her business. The joys of living in a small town... Except it didn't bother her anymore.

Sydney held out a hand. "Let me carry it for you. If you get one of these straps caught in your spokes, you'll wipe out."

Meagan passed it to her. "It's a little faded, but you can't beat the price."

When she got to the Tuckers' house, Darci's parents were loading suitcases into their car, preparing for a vacation in the mountains. Darci's mom called a friendly greeting as she headed back inside, but Darci's dad approached. He loved to talk. She was going to be there awhile.

She took the life jacket from Sydney and nodded down at Chandler. "You can finish his walk. I'll be fine the rest of the way."

After chatting with Mr. Tucker for several minutes,

Meagan left Darci's bike in the driveway and crossed the front yard. Just before she rounded the corner to head toward her boat, a Cedar Key police cruiser moved past, Hunter at the wheel.

Great. He would see she was alone, and scold her.

When she reached her boat, she took the pack off her back and laid it on the seat. With three cans of soup, a pound of butter and a half gallon of milk inside, it was rather heavy. But Darci's bicycle didn't have a basket. And her own had gotten crushed when Sally ran over her bike.

Relieved of her burden, Meagan inspected the life jacket more carefully, checking the seams and making sure the straps weren't damaged. When she finished, she glanced up to see Hunter stalking toward her. He was miffed. It was as obvious in his stormy expression as it was in his walk.

He planted his hands on his hips. "Where do you think you're going?"

"Nowhere."

He narrowed his gaze. "Don't give me that. You're leaving."

"No, I'm not."

He took a step closer, his eyes filled with suspicion. "You're standing at your boat holding on to a life jacket."

She stood her ground. "I'm holding a life jacket because someone was throwing it away, and I nabbed it."

"You promised you wouldn't leave. You're breaking that promise."

"I made a promise, and other than the one time I tried to leave to protect *your* sorry self, I've kept it. I'm not going anywhere except home."

"I don't believe you."

Anger surged through her. "You know what? I don't

have to justify my actions to you." She threw the life jacket into the boat on top of the other one and snatched up the pack. No matter what happened between her and Hunter, it would always be the same. She had lied to him when she'd first come to Cedar Key. She had lied to everyone. And though he had forgiven her, learning the truth had shattered his trust. And trust once lost was hard to win back. Especially for someone who saw everything black and white, like Hunter.

"If you weren't planning to leave, why are you packed?"

"What are you talking about?"

She started to swing the pack onto her back, then stopped. Her breath came out in a bitter laugh. Hunter's expression grew darker.

She glared at him. "I didn't pack anything. I went grocery shopping."

"What?"

She set the pack on the ground and unzipped it, revealing the items inside. "I had a few things to pick up at the grocery store, and since Darci's bike doesn't have a basket, I figured this would be the easiest way to get them home."

"You aren't supposed to be going anywhere alone." His tone was scolding, but a lot of the fire had left his eyes.

"I didn't go alone. Sydney was with me until ten minutes before you pulled up. Then it was Mr. Tucker. And if you'd like to follow me home, that will complete all the babysitting shifts."

The last of the fire left Hunter's eyes, replaced by meek apology. "I'm sorry, Meagan. I thought—"

"I know what you thought." He'd seen the life jacket and backpack and jumped to the worst conclusion without bothering to hear her out. And when she'd tried to explain, he hadn't believed her.

"Let me take you home."

"I'll ride. You can follow me if you'd like."

Once she arrived at the small white house, she carried the bike up the stairs onto the porch. Hunter was beside her before she could get inside.

"Meagan, I'm sorry. I—"

She held up a hand. "You have my trust, but you won't give me yours in return. Trust is a two-way street, you know." She pushed her key into the lock with a little more force than necessary. "Now go take your suspicions elsewhere. I'm heading inside."

She pushed open the door, but he held up a hand, blocking her entry. "Meagan, please wait. Hear me out."

After heaving an exasperated sigh, she turned to face him, arms crossed.

"I'm sorry I didn't believe you. I was wrong. This is no excuse, but I've been lied to all my life. Being distrustful is second nature." He stared down at her, his eyes pleading.

Tenderness tried to weave a path through her anger, but she slapped it aside. Hunter knew why she did what she did. But it didn't matter. He wasn't only holding her accountable for her own sins, he was holding her accountable for the sins of his family.

"I'm not your brother. Never will be."

She pushed her way past him and into the house. After stepping over the threshold, she closed and locked the door, then sank down on the couch, eyes closed.

Maybe she had overreacted. The problem was, she had fallen in love with Hunter Kingston. And she had secretly held out hope that maybe someday he would love her in return.

This morning's conversation had doused that hope completely. There would never be anything more than friendship between her and Hunter. It wasn't just his past—that he had fallen in love, planned his future, then had all his dreams ripped from him in an instant.

No, his problem was much more current. And more specific.

It was her.

Because no matter how she justified what she had done in the past, no matter how much she proved herself in the future, the ugly truth would stand.

She would never be good enough.

TEN

Meagan moved between two shelf units with quick swishes of the broom. In another fifteen minutes, she would close out the day's business. Darci had left some time ago.

But Meagan wasn't alone. A plainclothes detective had been hanging out in the store all day, the same as when Sally was making attempts on her life. Sally was no longer a threat. But Edmund was. Especially now that she had found the memory card and turned it over to the Napa Police Department.

The bell on the front door sounded, and she leaned the broom against the shelf and hurried to the front. It was Hunter.

"You're early. It's only five-thirty."

"I know." He glanced around. There were currently no customers in the store, but the detective was in the back. Hunter lowered his voice. "We didn't part on very good terms yesterday. It was totally my fault, and I'm sorry. I shouldn't have doubted you."

"No, you shouldn't have. I did what I had to do to survive. But that's not who I am. I'm straightforward. I keep my promises. And I don't lie."

"I know." His tone was still soft, his eyes filled with apology. "I was wrong. Forgive me?"

She heaved a sigh. She couldn't stay angry with him for long. Especially when he was looking at her like that, with such sincerity. She had done a lot of thinking, and while she understood where Hunter was coming from, his distrust didn't hurt any less. Neither did the fact that, no matter how much time they spent together, they would never be more than friends. But it wasn't Hunter's fault that she had fallen in love with him. He had done nothing to encourage her.

She gave him a weak smile. "Okay. You're off the hook this time."

His breath came out in a relieved sigh, which might have been a bit exaggerated. He leaned against the counter, his posture more relaxed than it had been since he entered the store.

"I have some news. We got a call from California. They've found the body."

Her pulse jumped to double time as hope coursed through her. "So Edmund has been arrested?"

"Not exactly. There's a warrant, but no one seems to know where he is."

Which meant he'd probably gotten wind of what was going on and was in hiding. Maybe he wasn't even in California. Maybe he was in Florida. In Cedar Key.

"We got some other good news, too. Eduardo Abelli flew in to San Francisco International Airport two days before Charlie was murdered, and flew back out a week later."

Meagan sagged against the counter in relief. Edmund's alibi. The final piece of the puzzle. "Eduardo took that plane to Maine using Edmund's passport."

"Yep. And since it appears that Eduardo had never flown to the US before, that's probably the conclusion a jury will come to also." Hunter frowned, and his eyes filled with worry. "Edmund is especially dangerous now. He's a man with nothing to lose. I wish I didn't have to let you out of my sight."

"It's not your full-time job to protect me." The fact that he wanted to sent warmth flooding her chest. But that was what he did. He was a hero, sworn to protect the innocent.

"I would if I could. But besides having a job to do, I've got a couple of things coming up that are going to take me away from Cedar Key. My dentist appointment I could cancel, but if I miss Amber's birthday dinner next week, she'll skewer me."

Meagan smiled. "Don't get in trouble with your sister. There are plenty of others keeping an eye on me."

"I'm hoping Edmund will be caught by then, anyway. He can't stay in hiding forever."

"No, but he could disappear to Italy and just lie low over there for a while."

"He'd never make it out of the country. He's a wanted man. If he tries to buy an airline ticket, it'll trigger an alert."

She nodded. That would be something that Edmund would probably know. He would find another way to get out of the States, maybe using Eduardo's passport. It wouldn't be that hard to have it overnighted.

But before he left, he would try to take care of some unfinished business. If he even knew he *had* unfinished business. If neither he nor Lou saw that news report, and no one mentioned who'd provided the memory card, Cedar Key wouldn't even be on his radar.

One way or another, this was soon going to be over. The authorities were closing in. Wherever Edmund was, his days of freedom were numbered.

While she finished her sweeping, then closed out the

day's business, Hunter chatted with the detective. At six o'clock, she met them both at the door. Hunter stepped outside ahead of her and waited while she locked up.

"What are you doing this evening?"

"Going home and chilling. The usual." She didn't have much of a social calendar. The engagements she had usually involved Hunter.

"Good." He opened the passenger door and helped her into his truck. "I want to take you to dinner. There's a warrant out for Edmund's arrest. They've got evidence that will stick. Sometime soon, he's going to be paying for his crimes. This is cause for celebration."

She frowned at him. "I think I'll pass. The last time you took me out to dinner to celebrate, I got kidnapped."

He cringed. "Good point. But we'll keep you out of the ladies' room this time. At least I won't let you go in without me checking every stall, then standing guard outside the door until you come back out."

She finally accepted his invitation, in spite of how the last time had turned out, and thirty minutes later they were seated at a table in Steamers, salad plates between them.

Hunter gave her a relaxed smile. "So what are you going to do once this is all over?"

"First? Call my mom."

Several times over the past few months, she had allowed the scenario to play through her mind—making that long-awaited phone call, hearing her mother's voice and telling her she was alive and why she had done what she had. That particular daydream always brought forward memories that were bittersweet. Each time, she relished all that she was feeling—the joy and the loss. Then scolded herself for engaging in impossible fantasies.

"And after that?"

"I really haven't thought beyond that. I never considered the possibility that there could ever come a day when Edmund would no longer be a threat." She took a long swig of her iced tea. "I guess I would go back to California." But if a certain Cedar Key police officer wanted to try to convince her otherwise, it wouldn't take much persuasion.

He gave a sharp nod. "I figured as much."

She sighed and beat back disappointment. There wouldn't be any convincing coming from Hunter. Whatever she felt for him, it wasn't returned. Which was fine. Because there was still the trust issue. And the fact that she would never have his.

She squared her shoulders and spoke with an enthusiasm she didn't feel. "I'll go back to my life as Elaina Thomas, try to pick up where I left off a few months ago. At the time I had to disappear, I was at the start of a pretty promising art career. I had just gotten several of my paintings into a prestigious gallery in New York."

"You definitely need to pursue that. You've got a lot of talent."

His compliment filled her with warmth, but before she had a chance to thank him, his phone began to ring. He swiped a finger across the screen and put it to his ear.

"Yeah, I'm with her now." His eyes widened, and his jaw dropped. "Thanks for letting me know. I'll tell her right away."

While he pocketed the phone, she leaned forward, body stiff with anticipation. "What?"

"That was Chief Sandlin. He just learned that Edmund's car was found burned up at the bottom of a cliff about fifteen miles northwest of his estate. He apparently lost control and ran off the road."

"Was he…inside?"

"There was one charred body at the wheel. They recovered a sterling silver necklace, which has been identified as belonging to Edmund."

"The Maori bird symbol."

"Yeah. It was damaged, some of the points had warped in the flames, but it was still recognizable."

The air whooshed out of her lungs, and she leaned back in her chair. Relief swept through her, followed by guilt. She frowned and looked at Hunter.

"I just heard about somebody's death, and all I feel is relief. Does that make me a horrible person?"

Understanding filled his eyes. "In this case, it's totally justifiable."

A slow smile crept up her cheeks. She couldn't stop it if she tried. A huge burden had just been lifted.

Freedom. It felt surreal. After moving through life with a chain around her throat for the past year and a half, she could hardly believe it was over.

When she looked back at Hunter, he was studying her with warmth in his eyes. "I love to see you smile." He reached across the table and took her hand. "After all you've been through, you deserve to be happy."

She laid her fork across her empty salad plate and met his gaze. His eyes were still warm, but there was something else there, an underlying sadness, maybe even longing. She squeezed his hand.

"And what about you? Are you happy?"

"Of course." He answered a little too quickly. "I have a good family, a job I love, great friends and an awesome church."

And no special someone to come home to every night. To share the little joys and successes. To hold his hand through the storms.

The same things that were lacking in her own life.

What would it take to win Hunter's love? Did she have the slightest chance? Did anyone?

The waitress arrived with their meals, shattering the seriousness of the moment. After some banter with Hunter and several friendly words for Meagan, she walked away with their empty salad plates. Hunter knew her well, said she attended his church. Of course, he seemed to know everyone.

Meagan peeled back the foil and slathered her baked potato with butter and sour cream. After swallowing her first bite of fish, she sat back in her chair and sighed. "It still seems surreal." She was half-afraid she would wake up and find out it was all a dream, that there was no disk and no body and no news that cast Edmund's alibi in doubt.

Hunter flashed her a smile. "It's probably going to take a few days to sink in."

"I'm sure. I almost wish I didn't have to work tomorrow. I think I'd go on a long bicycle ride through every street in Cedar Key. Then I'd get in my boat and motor up the coast with no destination in mind. I'd just savor the experience of being able to go where I want, when I want, without someone having to watch out for my safety."

Hunter frowned. "Don't let your guard down too much. I'm not going to rest easy until that body is positively identified with dental records."

Her elation ratcheted down several notches as doubt crept in. But it had to be Edmund. It was his car. And his jewelry. Although Lou often drove the Mercedes, he wouldn't wear Edmund's jewelry.

But Hunter was cautious. And he was concerned for her. That concern was one of the things that had endeared him to her. One of many. So she wouldn't add to his stress by being careless. She had stayed under the protection of law enforcement so many weeks now. What was a few more days?

When they arrived at her house, Hunter walked with her to the door.

"Make sure you lock this."

"Believe me, I will." She looked past him into the darkness. "Are the detectives still out there?"

"I'm sure of it."

She nodded. The thought was comforting, at least until they knew beyond a shadow of a doubt that Edmund was dead. She thanked Hunter for dinner, then wrapped her arms around his neck. A friendly hug was in line. But no more kisses. At least if she wanted to keep her sanity.

She watched him walk to his truck, then closed and locked the door. She hadn't invited him in. As always, she had enjoyed his company. But she had a phone call to make. She drew in a deep breath and tried to calm her suddenly racing heart. Trepidation, anticipation and joy all collided within her, and when she pulled her cell phone from her purse, her hand shook.

Her impossible fantasy was about to become a reality.

She dialed a familiar number, the same as she had a dozen times before. Except this time she pressed Send. It rang three times. Then a sweet feminine voice answered.

A wave of emotion washed over her, so powerful it took her breath away. She swallowed hard. "Mom?"

That was her last intelligible word. The maelstrom swirling inside her exploded in a series of sobs, fierce and uncontrollable.

She had her life back. And she had her family back. She would never take anything for granted again.

* * *

Meagan passed through the Tuckers' living room, picking up used paper bowls and a yellow sippy cup. It was almost eight forty-five, so Darci would be arriving at any moment. Meagan had actually expected her fifteen minutes ago.

They had all three arrived at church a half hour early. Upon getting out of the car, Jayden had thrown up. A hand on his forehead confirmed their fears—he was sick. With her parents out of town, and no one to teach her Wednesday-night class on such short notice, Darci was left in a bind.

Meagan was happy to help, and had had Darci drive them to her parents' house before church started. When faced with the two options, which task to volunteer for was a no-brainer. Taking care of one two-year-old had to be easier than teaching a half-dozen middle schoolers.

And it was. She and Jayden had spent a good bit of the evening eating chicken noodle soup and watching the Disney movie *Frozen*. At least *she* had watched it. Jayden's attention had bounced between the TV screen and the wide variety of toys that currently lay scattered about the living room.

After throwing the paper bowls away and setting the empty sippy cup in the sink, she returned to the living room to place a hand on Jayden's forehead. The fever that had confined him to home tonight seemed to be gone. His soup even stayed down.

He shook his head to brush her hand away. He was currently occupied with a toy laptop, chattering softly. Jayden didn't talk, but he did plenty of vocalizing—his own combination of sounds that only he understood.

She dragged a plastic tub into the center of the room. "Mommy's coming home soon. Let's pick up the toys."

Jayden continued his one-sided conversation without taking his eyes from the laptop. Meagan sighed. There was probably a way to engage him, and speaking from above wasn't it. She dropped to her hands and knees and put her face near his. "Hey, sweetie. Jayden?"

She apparently penetrated his world, because soft blue eyes met hers.

"Let's play the pickup game." She scooped up a teddy bear and started singing the same silly "cleanup" song her mother used to sing to her and her sister.

A sudden pang of homesickness shot through her, and she sighed. Three more days. Her mom and sister both were catching a flight out of California on Saturday.

Meagan dropped the teddy bear into the tub, and Jayden followed with a large rubber ball. The game seemed to be working…for about ten seconds. Two toys made it into the receptacle, then Jayden lost interest and returned to his laptop.

She had just scooped up the last toys when the doorbell rang. Darci had apparently forgotten her key. She actually lived in the apartment over her parents' garage, but when they were gone, she stayed in the house. It was much bigger, and there was no narrow staircase to navigate.

Before Meagan could drop the toys into the box and get to the foyer, Jayden sprang to his feet and padded in his socks to the front door. She hurried after him. He probably wasn't tall enough to reach the dead bolt, but she wasn't taking any chances. It would be a long time before the jumpiness left her.

She glanced through the sidelight window, and the tension left her shoulders. Darci's red Corolla sat in the drive. As soon as Meagan undid the lock, Jayden turned the doorknob and swung the door open.

The porch was empty.

Fear slid down her throat, turning to ice in her gut. A detective might be somewhere nearby, but it wasn't likely. One watched the store, and one watched her house. The rest of the time she was with other people. Before she could pull Jayden out of the doorway, a figure stepped away from the wall and into view.

A tall, slender, masculine figure.

Edmund.

She stood frozen as he pushed his way inside and scooped up Jayden in one smooth motion.

He kicked the door shut and twisted the lock. "You make a peep, and I snap his neck."

Her thoughts spun out of control. She needed to say something, but words wouldn't form. Edmund had found her. But that was impossible. He was dead. And it was Darci's car that sat in the driveway.

Horror washed through her, jarring her out of her stupor. Darci had gotten home. What had he done to her?

"Where is Darci?"

"The cute brunette? She was a feisty thing."

Was? Dear God, please, not Darci. "What did you do to her?"

"Don't worry, she won't interrupt any of our fun."

Meagan's knees almost buckled, and she grasped the wall for support. If Edmund hurt Darci, she would never forgive herself. She should have left Cedar Key weeks ago. Instead, she had let Hunter talk her into staying. Now she had led Edmund straight to Darci and Jayden.

But she had thought she was safe.

"You're supposed to be dead."

"That makes two of us. It's not so much fun being the deceived instead of the deceiver, is it?"

She shook her head, her thoughts swirling in a pool of confusion. "So who was in the car?"

"A homeless guy that Lou found passed out under a bridge. Once I learned the cops were looking for Patti's body, I knew I would have to disappear. Like I said, I took my cue from the best. Pretending to die worked pretty well for you until that news report aired. But there's a difference between you and me. *I'm* going to be smart enough to avoid the media."

His gaze was full of disdain. "You know, I recognized you immediately. You'd have to do a lot more than cut and color your hair to fool me."

Jayden pressed his hands against Edmund's chest and straightened his legs. When Edmund tightened his hold, the boy stiffened and his face began to redden. He was building up to a scream. Meagan had witnessed it before. An earsplitting, glass-shattering scream. A scream that Edmund would do anything to stop.

The realization stamped out the last of her shocked stupor.

"Put him down."

"You're in no position to make demands."

"He's going to scream. Put him down, and he'll be quiet."

Indecision flashed across Edmund's face. But only for a second. Then he bent and let the boy slide out of his arms. The moment Jayden's feet touched the floor, he ran behind her and wrapped himself around one of her legs. He was counting on her to protect him. Unfortunately, she couldn't even protect herself.

Edmund reached into the pocket of the lightweight jacket he wore and pulled out a rope and a small roll of duct tape. "Gag him and tie him up."

Her eyes widened. He had come prepared. Of course,

she wouldn't expect anything less from Edmund. He was meticulous in everything he did.

She took the items from him.

"Don't look so shocked. I've been watching you for the past week and a half."

Since the pirate festival. She hadn't been mistaken. That *was* Lou and Edmund she saw. Lou had apparently gone back home. Edmund hadn't.

"Now get on with it." He nudged her toward the kitchen. "I've waited a long time for this night. Get the kid taken care of so we can start the party." His tone was hard as flint, with a cruel edge.

Hopelessness descended on her. There was no way out. Any desperate attempts at escape would put Jayden at risk. Whatever happened to her, she had to save him.

"You can do what you want to me. Just don't hurt the boy. He has nothing to do with this."

"That depends on how well you cooperate. And how well he stays quiet."

She lifted Jayden into one of the dining-room chairs, then got down on her knees in front of him.

"We're going to play a game. Good guys and bad guys." She wasn't sure how much he understood, but for once she seemed to have his full attention. "Edmund and Miss Meagan are bad guys. We're going to tie you up, and then Mommy is going to rescue you."

Dear God, please let it be true. If Darci was just unconscious somewhere, or tied up and gagged where someone might find her, there could be a chance. But no help was likely to come tonight. Unless…

Hunter had spent the afternoon with his family, then gone to dinner. If it wasn't too late when he got home, maybe he would check on her.

"Tape his mouth first. I don't want any sounds out of him."

She tore off a three-inch piece of the tape and held it up. "Are you ready? Here we go." She pressed the tape against his face, careful to leave his nose exposed.

Jayden began to jerk his head back and forth and push her away. When he tried to tear at the tape, Edmund nudged her with the barrel of a gun. It had apparently been in the jacket. "You get him under control, or I will."

Panic shot through her. Surely he wouldn't shoot Jayden, would he? She wouldn't put anything past him.

She held the tiny wrists together with one hand while looping the rope and tightening it with her other, assisting with her teeth when necessary. When he resisted, she tightened her grip. Big tears welled up in his eyes, overflowing to run down both cheeks.

Her heart twisted. Jayden didn't understand. And there was no way to explain it to him. In his little two-year-old mind, Miss Meagan was being mean. Miss Meagan didn't love him anymore.

Before she straightened, she brushed a soft kiss on his cheek. "I'm sorry, sweetie." She spoke the words in a whisper right next to his ear.

"Now bring the rope around and tie him to the chair."

She did as told, then turned to face Edmund. She had done everything he asked. Jayden was restrained, and except for some muffled whimpers, he was quiet. But that didn't mean Edmund wouldn't kill him when he was finished with her. In fact, chances were good that he wouldn't leave alive anyone who could identify him.

But Jayden wouldn't identify him. Maybe if Edmund knew that, Jayden would be safe. "The boy is autistic and doesn't talk. He's no threat to you."

"Then maybe I'll let him live. That's dependent on your behavior. The ball's in your court, babe."

She inwardly cringed at his use of the pet name. But maybe she could play it to her advantage. Maybe somewhere beneath that twisted thirst for vengeance was a spark of whatever it was that had drawn him to her to begin with.

"Let me come home. We can work things out." She would rather go back with Edmund than risk harm to Jayden.

Edmund gave a derisive snort. "If you would have changed your mind and come back to me right away, that might have worked. It's much too late for that now."

He gripped a handful of her hair and jerked her head back. His left hand still held the gun. "Do you have any idea what I've gone through these last few months? Two fiancées in four years. That doesn't look good. And I didn't even have anything to do with it this time." He relaxed his grip on her hair. "Now, turn out the lights, all except the hall light. And make it quick."

She flipped several switches, throwing first the dining room, the kitchen, then the living room into darkness. A hand wrapped around her upper arm, tightening with a steel-like grip, and she bit off a startled cry. He propelled her down the hall to the open doorway to Darci's parents' bedroom. Then he released her and shoved her into the room, so hard that she landed on her hands and knees. The door closed, and the lock clicked behind them. What was he going to do to her?

Whatever he had in mind, at least it wouldn't be in front of Jayden. He would have enough trauma from this night without watching Edmund take his revenge. If he even let the boy live.

Edmund again grabbed a fistful of her hair, and a

startled cry surged up her throat as he hauled her to her feet. Pain shot through her scalp and neck. She stumbled ahead of him, his hand propelling her forward, past the bed and into the bathroom. For the third time a door closed and the lock clicked into place.

"Do you know why we're here?"

"No." A terrifying possibility gnawed at the edges of her mind, but she refused to voice it, refused to even let it solidify into a coherent thought.

"Look around." He released his hold on her. "What do you see?"

A modern bathroom in a sixty- or seventy-year-old house, complete with his-and-hers vanities, a whirlpool tub large enough for two, a walk-in shower and a separate water closet. Darci's parents had spared no expense on their renovations.

"Still don't know?"

She shook her head, trying to dispel the image that was wrapping itself around her mind.

"Let me give you a hint. How did you leave me?"

"I took your boat."

"You faked your own death." He nailed her with an ominous glare. "By drowning."

A sheet of perspiration coated her palms, and her heart began an erratic rhythm. She had faked her death by drowning, and that was how Edmund planned to kill her.

"Start filling the tub."

Cold terror rained down on her, slowly turning every cell in her body to stone. He had given her a command. But her mind wouldn't will her body to act.

"I said start filling the tub." Anger underscored each word.

She knew better than to disobey him. She had learned

that lesson long before leaving California. But horror held her rooted to the spot.

Edmund grabbed her by the hair again and shoved her toward the door.

"Wh-what are you doing?"

"I'm going to start with the boy. And you're going to watch."

"No!" Panic pushed aside the fear that had held her immobile. She tried to comply with Edmund's earlier order, but he didn't release his grip on her hair.

"I'll fill the tub. I'll do whatever you ask. Just leave Jayden out of it."

For several tense moments, her captor didn't move. Finally, he leaned close to her ear. "I'm giving you one more chance. You blow it again, and you forfeit the kid's life. Understand?"

She nodded and stumbled to the tub. She would do anything to save that sweet, innocent little boy. Even if it meant letting Edmund drown her. She turned the dial to plug the drain and turned on first the cold, then the hot water.

But as the tub began to fill, that temporary strength she had found began to waver. The sound of running water was supposed to be soothing. Instead, it had become a death knell.

She once again tried to quell the panic stabbing through her.

"Why don't you just shoot me?" Anything would be better than drowning.

"No, this is perfect. I call it poetic justice. You let the world believe you had drowned. This time it's going to be real."

God, please send someone. Please don't let this be the end.

She closed her eyes. It would take at least ten minutes for the tub to fill enough for Edmund to do what he wanted to do.

Please let someone get here in time.

Even as she prayed, she didn't hold out much hope. The Tuckers were out of town for another week. And no one was likely to drop by at nine o'clock on a Wednesday night.

Unless Hunter came. And he *would*. Eventually. When he couldn't get a hold of either Darci or her, he would come looking for them. But would he get there in time? And if he did, would he be able to save her and Jayden?

Or would Edmund get to him first?

"Climb in." Edmund's voice cut into her spinning thoughts.

Her gaze shot to the tub, which was still filling. The water was only about six inches deep. "Already?"

Anger flared in his eyes. "If you're thinking about standing here and arguing with me, we'll go get the kid."

"No." The word came out loud and sharp, with much more strength than she was feeling. Edmund was going to drown her. And unlike her ordeal with Sally Ferguson, she couldn't even resist. If she did, Jayden would die.

She put one foot on the tile step. The other one followed. Then she bent and rested both hands on the edge of the tub, balancing herself as she swung one leg over the side.

"Hurry it up. I don't have all night."

He gave her a push and she fell sideways, cracking her head on the opposite edge. Unfortunately, it wasn't hard enough to knock her out. That would have been preferable. She could have slipped into oblivion, relaxed and unaware as water filled her lungs.

Instead, she would experience every agonizing moment, fully and completely.

Edmund gripped the back of her neck, and panic shot through her. It was starting. And there was nothing she could do but submit.

But as he began to press her face toward the water, every muscle tensed of its own accord. She was on her hands and knees, her elbows locked. The tub continued to fill, the sound of the rushing water fraying the last of her nerves. If she didn't cooperate, Edmund would kill Jayden. But she couldn't overcome the terror that had gripped her.

Suddenly, Edmund's hold on her relaxed and he heaved a sigh. "So you're going to make me go get the kid."

Her throat constricted, and her heart threatened to explode through her chest. "No." She would do whatever she had to do to protect Jayden. "I'm lying down right now."

With Edmund's hand still resting on the back of her neck, she slid her knees away from her hands, until her hips rested on the bottom of the tub, then slowly bent her elbows. Finally, she sucked in a huge breath of air, filling her lungs to capacity. How long could one go without breathing? One minute? Two?

If she stayed calm, she would be able to hold out longer. Whatever happened, she couldn't resist. She had to submit.

But as her face dipped beneath the surface, all thoughts about remaining calm fled. Renewed panic pounded through her. She couldn't do this.

But she had to. For Jayden.

She reined in her spiraling thoughts and once again willed herself to relax. By holding her breath, she was only delaying the inevitable. No one was coming. There was no one to help her.

But the longer she held on, the more time she gave Darci's little boy. Edmund had said he wouldn't hurt him if she cooperated. Chances were good that he was lying.

If Hunter can't get here in time to save me, please let him save Jayden.

Hunter blew through the stop sign at Fifth and G, slowing just enough to check for traffic. Worry pulled every muscle in his body taut. He'd been trying to reach Meagan, and each time, the call went to voice mail. Maybe her phone was on vibrate.

The problem was, he had tried to call Darci several times and had had the same experience. What were the odds that they *both* had their phones on vibrate?

When he left for Ocala early that afternoon, he'd been confident that Meagan would be safe. A detective would be with her at the store. Then she was going from work to church with Darci, and having Blake take her home. And a detective would be watching her house.

Except she never made it home.

Actually, she never made it to church, either. According to Blake, she had volunteered to babysit a sick Jayden so Darci could teach her class.

Hunter whipped into the Tuckers' drive and jammed on the brakes. If Darci and Meagan were inside chatting, their phones silenced, he would shake them both. If not, he would call 911. He wasn't handling this alone.

He jammed the transmission into Park and scanned his surroundings. Darci's car was there, but the house was dark. The worry swirling through him congealed into a solid knot of fear. Darci and Meagan wouldn't be sitting inside conversing without lights. Something was terribly wrong.

He pulled his weapon from the console and jumped from the truck. After calling for backup, he jogged toward the house. A thud sounded next to him, and he spun, weapon raised. No one was there. Then a series of thuds came from Darci's trunk.

Realization slammed into him. His greatest fear was coming to pass. Edmund had found Meagan and was at that very moment inside with her. Darci would have to wait. For the time being, she was safe, albeit a little uncomfortable.

Meagan and Jayden weren't. For them, seconds could count. Backup would arrive shortly. And judging from the concern in his friend's voice when Hunter had talked to him minutes earlier, Blake would be among them.

But Hunter couldn't wait. He tried the front door, then circled the house, peering in windows, trying to figure out his best course of action. Lacy curtains hung behind the glass, the heavier drapes pulled back on each side.

When he reached the dining room window, the back porch light cast a soft glow into the room. There was a small figure in one of the chairs. Jayden. He sat in profile, but his head was turned away, leaning against the back of the chair. Something trailed around his hip. Was that rope? Was he tied to the chair?

Then Jayden's head turned toward him. Duct tape covered the lower portion of his face. Hunter clenched his fists as anger surged through him. If he could get his hands on Edmund at that moment, he would punch him in the face for touching Jayden. Then he would break one bone in his body for each and every time he had hurt Meagan.

He closed his eyes and willed himself to calm down.

God, help me handle this correctly. He needed to keep a clear head.

So where were Meagan and Edmund? Hunter jogged the rest of the way around the house, looking in windows. The bedroom ones had shades. That had to be where they were. What was Edmund doing to her? Whatever it was, something told him her time was running out.

He hurried back to the rear door and kicked it in. Jayden looked at him with wide, fear-filled eyes, and he gave him a reassuring smile, trying to convey to him that everything would be all right. Hopefully, he would be able to keep that unspoken promise.

He slipped down the hall, his sneakers hardly making a sound against the tile floor. Two bedroom doors were open. The third was closed. All was silent except...the sound of running water.

Panic pounded up his spine. Edmund was trying to drown her. She had faked her death by drowning, so that was the death he had chosen for her.

Hunter tried the knob, hoping to at least have the element of surprise on his side. It was locked. If Edmund was smart, he'd locked the bathroom door, too.

Hunter stepped back. If he couldn't have surprise, he would have speed. He charged across the room and threw his body against the door, then hit the second one without breaking his momentum.

The scene in front of him played out so quickly, he barely had time to react. Edmund was on his knees in front of the tub. He snatched his gun, sprang to his feet and spun around. Meagan rose up, gasping and coughing. A gunshot exploded in Hunter's ear, accompanied by a searing pain in his right upper arm. His weapon fell to the floor, and he dived for it, grabbing it with his other hand. Could he fire left-handed and not risk hitting Meagan?

Edmund didn't leave him a choice. He was already preparing to take a second shot. At the same moment, Meagan sprang to her feet and snatched a metal vase from the back corner of the tub. In one smooth motion, she stepped over the side and swung with both hands, bringing the vase down hard on Edmund's head. He staggered forward and dropped to his knees. His weapon discharged, the bullet lodging in the door casing a few inches from Hunter's head.

Now Edmund was far enough from the tub that Meagan was well out of harm's way. Hunter raised his weapon and aimed it at the man's chest. But he didn't have to shoot. Edmund's arm dropped and the pistol clattered to the floor. His eyes rolled back in his head, and he fell face-first onto the tile.

Hunter laid his weapon on the nearest counter and leaned against the doorjamb, trying to steel himself against the pain that seemed to rack his entire right side. Blackness encroached, and somewhere behind him, footsteps sounded. Backup had arrived.

Meagan climbed from the tub and hurried toward him, slipping and sliding on the wet tile. She threw herself into his arms. Or one, anyway. His right hung limp at his side. This shot had done more damage than the arrow had.

Hunter's knees gave out, and he began to slide down the doorjamb. Strong arms caught him from behind and eased him to the floor. Darkness closed in further, wiping out the last of the light, and the voices around him faded, then disappeared altogether.

His last conscious thoughts were that Meagan was finally safe.

And that he was bleeding all over the Tuckers' new tile.

ELEVEN

There was so much blood.

And she wasn't good with blood.

Meagan pressed a fist to her mouth and fought back nausea. Joe had eased Hunter to the floor and was working on getting him stabilized until the ambulance could arrive. The best thing she could do for him was to stay out of Joe's way.

Her eyes shifted to Gary, then to Steve, another Cedar Key officer. They had just stepped around Hunter and Joe and were putting handcuffs on Edmund.

She dropped her hand from her mouth and crossed her arms. She was dripping wet and starting to shiver. "Did you guys find Darci?"

Gary's eyes widened. "Is she missing?"

"She came home but never made it inside. Edmund got to her first."

The concern that flashed across Gary's face put a solid knot of fear in her gut. *God, please let her be okay.*

And please let Hunter be okay. If he lost too much blood, or if his arm was damaged beyond repair… It was his dominant arm. He could be permanently injured. And it would be her fault. She had left California to escape danger, and instead had brought it with her.

Gary dashed out the door and down the hall, where he met Blake coming in from the living room. They almost collided.

Blake held up a hand. "You got the lockout kit?"

Gary cocked a brow. "Sure do. Why?"

"We've got someone who needs it. I heard noise coming from the trunk of the Corolla, like someone was inside. I knocked and hollered, and no one answered, but the thumps got louder and faster. As tiny as that trunk is, I'm guessing it's Darci in there. You couldn't fit someone like me or you in that suitcase-sized space."

Instead of following them, Meagan continued to the dining room. When she flipped on the light and approached Jayden, fear filled his eyes. She pushed her still dripping hair away from her face and dropped to her knees in front of him. He shrank away from her, kicking his feet.

"It's okay, sweetie. Miss Meagan won't hurt you. Miss Meagan is going to rescue you. We're not going to play this game anymore."

She reached for the tape. Okay, this *would* hurt. "I'm going to take the tape off your face. It's going to sting when I do, but not for long. Then I'm going to untie you and take you to Mommy." Once she knew for sure that Mommy was okay.

Meagan grasped a corner of the tape and pulled, wincing in sympathy as she did. Jayden squeezed his eyes shut and drew in a deep breath. Then he let out an ear-piercing, bone-jarring scream. It wasn't the scream of frustration so common among autistic children. It was a scream of pure terror.

As she untied the ropes, she tried to soothe him. But nothing she said penetrated. He alternated between sobbing and screaming, until her own frayed nerves were ready to snap. Before she could get the rope untied from his wrists, he squirmed out of her grasp and ran down the hall and into the master suite.

Where Hunter was lying unconscious and bleeding. And where Edmund lay facedown on the floor, also unconscious and likely with a bloody nose.

She ran after him. He didn't need any more trauma tonight. She caught up to him in the doorway of the bathroom and scooped him up, gasping when her cold, wet T-shirt molded against her stomach. As she hurried down the hall toward the front of the house, he put up as much of a fight as his little body could muster, all the while continuing to scream and sob.

By now, Gary would have Darci's car open. The Cedar Key Police Department had a lockout kit and regularly helped tourists and residents who locked their keys in their cars. According to Hunter, they hadn't found a car yet that they couldn't get into. An older Toyota Corolla would be a piece of cake.

When she stepped onto the front porch, Gary was standing at Darci's open driver's door, bent at the waist, as if looking for the trunk release. Apparently he found it, because it suddenly exploded open. Blake stood at the back, ready to assist.

Meagan sprinted down the porch steps and hit the driveway at a run. Judging by the force with which Darci had kicked that trunk open, she wasn't incapacitated. And Jayden needed his mother.

When Meagan reached the car, Darci was sitting up, but her mouth was taped and her hands were tied behind her back. Her ankles were bound, too. Blake pulled the tape from her face.

Jayden's screams immediately stopped, but the sobs intensified. He leaned so far to the side, arms outstretched toward his mother, that Meagan was afraid she would drop him.

"It's okay, baby." Darci's voice cracked. "Mommy's okay. And you're okay."

As soon as Blake untied her hands and feet, Darci sprang out of the trunk and grasped her son. For several moments she crooned in his ear, rocking back and forth, until his sobs became nothing more than jagged breaths. Finally, he rested against her shoulder, and she looked at them past his little blond head.

"It was Edmund, wasn't it? I didn't even see him. I had just gotten out of my car. Before I could close the door, someone grabbed me from behind, wrapped his arm around my neck and squeezed."

She put a hand to her throat and shook her head. "He wasn't strangling me. I could still breathe. But within a few seconds everything went black."

Blake frowned. "I think you experienced a wrestler's choke hold."

"Whatever it was, the next thing I remember is waking up in the dark, bound and gagged. It took me a few minutes to figure out where I was." Creases settled between her brows, and her eyes locked with Meagan's. "I was sure Edmund was the one who attacked me, and all I could think about was that you and Jayden were inside with him."

Two ambulances arrived, and first Hunter, then Edmund were brought out. Hunter was now conscious. Edmund wasn't. Meagan had put more strength behind that blow than she'd realized.

She moved to the gurney carrying Hunter. His tanned face was blanched and lined with pain. Guilt stabbed through her. "I'm so sorry. This is my fault."

He reached for her hand as she walked beside him. "I

know I'm a little out of it, but I thought it was Edmund who did this."

Warmth filled her chest, accompanied by longing. Despite everything that had happened tonight, he could still tease her.

But she wasn't letting herself off the hook that easily. "If I had gone ahead and left when I was planning to, you wouldn't have gotten hurt."

The paramedics stopped at the open doors of the ambulance, but Hunter didn't release her hand. "If you remember, I'm the one who brought you back. So if my getting hurt is anyone's fault other than Edmund's, it would have to be mine."

She gave him a weak smile. "You saved my life. Thank you."

"And you saved mine. So we're even." He tried to return her smile, but his was more of a grimace. "You're pretty dangerous with a vase. Remind me to never make you mad."

He dropped her hand and the paramedics loaded him into the back of the ambulance.

"I'm getting a ride to the hospital." She hollered the words just before the doors closed, then stepped back and crossed her arms. She was even colder than before. Now her teeth were chattering. Whether from being soaking wet, or in a delayed reaction to almost dying tonight, she wasn't sure. But she was chilled all the way to the core.

She needed to get into some dry clothes. Then maybe she could get Blake to take her to the hospital. The doctors likely wouldn't let her see Hunter for some time. He would probably have to have surgery, at least to have the bullet removed. He might even have to have reconstructive surgery on the arm, a pin inserted if there was damage to the bone.

Whatever would have to be done, she would be there when he awoke. Because regardless of what he said, his injury was her fault.

But more than anything, she would be there for him because she loved him.

Once he recovered, she would have decisions to make. Such as whether to remain in Cedar Key, seeing Hunter on a regular basis, hoping that he would somehow come to feel the same way about her that she felt about him. Or accepting the fact that she and Hunter were destined to be nothing more than good friends. Or giving up on life in Cedar Key altogether and moving back to California.

Those were the decisions she would have to face eventually.

But not tonight. Tonight she would remember the kiss on his boat and how cherished she had felt in those moments. And how he often looked at her with emotion swimming in his blue eyes.

She clasped her hands and brought them to her chest. Yes, tonight she would hold on to that warmth.

And cling to her impossible dreams.

Moody.

That was how Meagan would describe Hunter over these past two weeks. And uncomfortable. At least around her.

The problem was, he knew how she felt about him. At least he had to have a strong suspicion. She never was that good at hiding her emotions. And now that she had become part of his inner circle—Blake, Allison, Sydney, Wade and Darci—he couldn't avoid her.

But he didn't have anything to worry about. She wasn't stalker material. She wouldn't try to force someone to feel something for her that wasn't there, no matter how much she cared for him. She would just quietly walk away.

And that was exactly what she was doing.

She sighed and placed the small stack of folded clothes into one side of the duffel bag. She was leaving with all the items she'd come with, plus some art supplies, her camera and a few extra changes of clothes.

But, she had traded the fear and uncertainty for an overwhelming sense of loss. Which was ridiculous. She couldn't lose something she'd never had.

Last night at church, she had said goodbye to everyone. There had been lots of hugs and more than a few tears. Even Jayden had given her a tentative wave. She hadn't been able to coax a hug from him. But that was okay. Since his ordeal, he had been exceptionally clingy, only turning loose of Darci to go to her mother. Hopefully, in time, he would forget. He was only two.

Amidst all the goodbyes, though, Hunter had stood silently to the side, his blue eyes impossible to read. She had hoped he would try to talk her into staying. It wouldn't have taken much.

But he hadn't. She shouldn't have expected anything different. It wasn't just losing his fiancée. It was the fact that Hunter had impossibly high standards. And she didn't meet them.

She stuffed the last of her belongings into her bag, then laid the house key on the counter and went to wait on the porch. The cab would arrive any minute to take her to the bus station. But there was one person who deserved a special final goodbye on her way out.

When Meagan walked into Darci's Collectibles and Gifts, her throat tightened. Darci had been so much more than an employer.

"I couldn't leave without saying bye one more time. Thank you for everything you've done for me."

Darci came out from behind the counter and wrapped her in a crushing hug that belied her small size. "I wish you didn't have to go. But I understand why. Your mom and sister are going to be happy to have you home."

Yes, they would be. At the time they came to visit, she hadn't yet decided whether she would stay. And not knowing when they would see each other again, they had all cried when they'd parted at the bus station.

Darci frowned. "I had really hoped that you and Hunter would get together. He cares about you. A lot. In the four years I've known him, this is the first time anyone has gotten past his barriers."

"A lot of good it's done. I believe his mind understands that I was left with no choice, but his heart can't get past the fact that I lied to him. He'll never fully trust me. Even if he did decide to give a relationship a try, I can't live like that."

"I don't blame you. I couldn't, either." Darci stepped forward and gave her another hug. When she released her, there were tears in her eyes. "You're going to find a church when you get home, right?"

"Definitely. And I'm going to stay in touch. Who knows? Maybe someday I'll find my way back to Cedar Key, at least for a vacation."

As Meagan walked out the door and got into the cab, she was fighting back tears herself. In a little over four months, Darci had become closer to her than any of her childhood friends. And she hadn't just grown to love Darci and Hunter and the others. She had grown to love Cedar Key itself—the quaintness, the tranquility, the Old Florida charm. The thought of going away left her with a big hole in her heart.

The cabdriver turned into the parking lot of the bus station and eased to a stop. After paying the fare, Meagan removed her items from the car—her purse, backpack and duffel bag, all her worldly possessions. Now that she was going to be able to put down deep roots, she could start acquiring some comforts of life rather than just the bare necessities.

As she approached the ticket counter, the clerk looked up, and her eyes lit with recognition, followed by disappointment. "I guess it didn't work out."

"No, I'm afraid it didn't."

"Sorry to hear that. He seemed like a nice young man."

Yeah, too nice.

"So where to?"

"Napa, California."

Meagan paid for the ticket, then settled onto a chair to read. The bus wouldn't leave for another three hours. She glanced at the door. No, Hunter wasn't going to show up this time. He'd come after her the first time because he had a case to solve. Now everything was neatly wrapped up. And he was ready to go back to his ordered life. No, today no one would stop her.

She pulled a paperback book out of her duffel and frowned at the cover. It was a romantic suspense. She had lived enough suspense during the past few months to last a lifetime. And romance? Well, she just wasn't in the mood.

Instead, she chose the book of poetry that had belonged to Charlie. Maybe it would help keep her mind off Hunter. Soon she would be on her way, each minute carrying her closer to the life she had left four and a half months ago, a life she'd never thought she would see again.

She had her family. She had her career. The future looked bright. Once she crossed the Florida border, she would feel that she had left Cedar Key and its memories behind. Then she would be ready to embrace the future.

A future without Hunter.

Hunter eased to a stop on Dock Street, his boat trailing behind the Tundra. A family of tourists crossed in front of him. After a slow September, the cooler October weather was bringing more activity to Cedar Key, which helped everybody, including Darci.

The small group stepped up onto the sidewalk and headed toward the Island Trader gift shop. Hunter pressed the gas and sighed. The omelet he'd had for breakfast sat like a rock in his gut.

Meagan was gone. He'd seen her leave. At least, he'd seen a cab stop at the curb in front of Darci's store and had watched her climb in. She didn't notice him. He was sitting at a stop sign a block away, waiting to cross Second. Even though traffic was clear, he didn't budge. He sat for several seconds staring at her, trying to imprint her image on his mind, until a horn had sounded behind him.

By now she would be at the bus station, ready to head back to her life in California. It was for the best. He really didn't know what he wanted. And she had her own issues. She needed time to heal.

He reached the end of Dock Street and followed the curve around to the left, headed toward the city boat ramp. As he drew closer, he spotted Blake sitting on a bench looking his way, his right leg extended and his cane propped against the seat next to him. What was *he* doing there? He had a boat of his own, a really nice one.

So sitting at the city ramp watching boaters come and go wasn't a usual pastime for him.

Hunter backed his boat down the ramp, and by the time he stepped out of the truck, Blake had made his way onto the dock. He stood with his arms crossed, leaning against the metal railing.

"I figured you'd show up."

"What do you mean?"

"Any time something's bothering you and you need to clear your head, you take the boat out."

Hunter stepped into the water to unhook the winch cable from the boat. "What makes you think something's bothering me? I can't work right now. I figured I'd go fishing."

"Uh-huh. So where is Meagan?"

"I assume she's at the bus station."

"You let her leave." It was a statement, not a question, but it was filled with disbelief. And a good dose of disgust.

"Of course I let her leave. What was I supposed to do, arrest her?" He stepped onto the dock, holding the bow line. He had to do everything left-handed, because his right was pretty much useless. A cast ran from his shoulder to below his elbow, and inside, a pin and screws held the bone together. And Blake seemed more prepared to harass than help.

"No, but you could have told her you wanted her to stay."

Hunter guided the boat off the trailer, then squatted to tie the line to a cleat. "What if I don't want her to stay?"

"That question doesn't even deserve a response."

Blake was right. It didn't. He wanted Meagan to stay as much as he had ever wanted anything. But to ask her would involve making promises he wasn't sure he could keep. Maybe not in so many words, but the implications would be there.

He had thought about it and prayed about it and agonized over the decision until it had almost driven him crazy.

He moved up the dock and got into his truck. "It doesn't matter whether I want her to stay. She has a life in California. Now that Edmund is going to be put away for a long time, she has no reason not to go back. What she does with her life is none of my concern."

"If Meagan's staying or leaving wasn't a big deal to you, you wouldn't have been so grouchy the past two weeks."

"I haven't been grouchy." He closed the door and stepped on the gas to pull the trailer up the ramp. After parking the truck, he returned to the dock.

Blake nailed him with a judgmental glare. "You want to know what your problem is?"

Hunter stepped onto the boat and moved to the back to start the motor. "No, but I'm sure you're going to tell me, anyway."

"You're in love with her, but you're too thickheaded and proud to see it."

"Pride doesn't have anything to do with it."

"Yes, it does. You've spent your whole life wrapped up in always being the *good* son, nothing like your brother."

Hunter scowled at Blake. He was the only one in Cedar Key who knew about Howard, and he was using it against him.

His friend obviously wasn't finished. "I know you don't want to hear this, but someone needs to tell you. You're so concerned about your squeaky-clean reputation, not one woman in a thousand is going to be perfect enough to meet your standards."

"Look, I'm not just thinking of me. I'm thinking of her, too."

"How?"

"Now that Edmund is no longer a threat, she'll ditch the alias and go back to her real name. How do you think the people of Cedar Key will take to being deceived for the past several months?" Everything she had presented them with had been a lie. How would they ever trust her? How could *he* ever trust her?

"The people of Cedar Key will be reasonable enough to see that she had no choice. And they'll admire her courage and strength and ingenuity."

"Maybe that's true. But I'm responsible for setting an example for my kids." He had drilled it into them how important integrity was. To always tell the truth, even when it was hard. He had standards to maintain, both as a mentor to young people and an officer of the law.

He untied the dock line, then kicked the motor into reverse. Even though he was moving away, Blake's words still reached him.

"Someone was trying to kill her, so she changed her name, just like they do in witness protection. Now she's changing it back. It's not a big deal."

Hunter backed away from the dock, then shifted to forward. Blake managed one more comment.

"Face it. You're the only one with a problem."

He gunned it and sped away from the ramp. Maybe he was. But his problem wasn't pride. It was trust. Being repeatedly lied to had a tendency to make one leery of believing what others said.

He had never set out to be "the good son." He had ended up with the title by default. Almost from the time they could walk, Howard had seemed bent on destruction. And had caused their parents countless hours of grief.

Hunter had always tried to be as good as his brother was bad. Praise was a great motivator. So, unlike Howard, he towed the line, always took the right path and never got into trouble.

And he was mighty proud of it.

He pulled back on the throttle as realization broadsided him. Was that what Blake was talking about? Was he really proud? And was that pride making him so judgmental of others that he didn't consider Meagan good enough for him?

Or was he, as Blake said, so concerned about his great reputation that he didn't want to consider hooking up with someone who might have a few blemishes on theirs?

With Denise, it hadn't been an issue. She was a pastor's daughter, raised in the church, well thought of in the community, known for her transparency.

Since her death, he hadn't been willing to love again. But now, for the first time in four years, he was ready. Something had happened over the past few weeks, so gradual he hadn't noticed the change. Healing had begun.

Was Meagan the one? He didn't know.

But one thing was certain. If he let her go back to California, he would never find out.

Time moved at a snail's pace.

Meagan sighed and dropped her gaze from the clock on the wall to the book of poetry lying open in her lap. Voices buzzed around her, and across the room, a mother tried to quiet a crying baby.

The door opened, but she refused to lift her head. She

had spent the past hour and a half looking up in anticipation every time someone opened the bus station door,
then drowning in disappointment when it turned out to
be yet another stranger.

No more. It was time to face the stark truth. Hunter
wasn't coming.

She turned the page, to "Twenty Years Hence," by
Walter Savage Landor.

A figure stepped into her peripheral vision and drew
closer. Probably another passenger waiting for his de-
parture time.

Twenty years hence my eyes may grow,
If not quite dim, yet rather so...

It was a man wearing shorts and tennis shoes. She
could tell that much without her eyes leaving the page.
He approached and sat immediately to her right. With
all the empty chairs in the place, he had to choose the
one right next to her?

Yet yours from others they shall know,
Twenty years hence.

A familiar scent wafted toward her, the faintest hint
of evergreen, tipped with spice. Her thoughts tumbled
over one another.

"Mind if I interrupt your reading?" The voice close
to her ear was liquid smooth, sending goose bumps cas-
cading over her.

She squelched the unexpected urge to throw herself
into his arms, and instead rested her hands on the book,
fingers entwined. "What are you doing here?"

"I came to ask you to stay."

"I've already bought my ticket."

"You can turn it in."

She shifted in her chair to angle herself toward him.
Ever since she had decided to leave, she had wanted

nothing more than for Hunter to ask her to stay. Now that he was doing just that, she was no longer sure. He had given her no indication that he felt anything deeper than friendship for her. If it was all going to lead to a dead end, she would be better off leaving now.

"Why? Why do you want me to stay?"

He glanced around him, and she followed his gaze. No one seemed interested in their business. No one except the clerk. She was the same one who had been at the ticket counter the last time. She currently had no customers and sat staring at them, one ear cocked. She wasn't even trying to be inconspicuous.

Hunter shifted in his chair. "Can we talk outside?"

She shrugged. "Whatever you have to say, I don't see any reason why it can't be said right here."

He looked around again. They had garnered the attention of a couple other people. "Come on, Meagan, let's go outside."

"You're way too concerned about what everyone thinks of you. You want me to stay? Prove it."

He heaved a sigh, full of resignation, and his eyes locked with hers. "Yes, I want you to stay. I want you to stay, because if you leave, I'm afraid I'll never see you again. And I don't know that I could live with that."

"And if I stay?"

"I don't know." His gaze shifted to the opposite wall. For several long moments he was silent, the struggle inside evident on his face.

And she waited. He didn't have to commit to forever. *She* wasn't ready to commit to forever. But he had to at least be willing to give it a shot. She wasn't going to stay in Cedar Key to be just another one of Hunter's friends. She had friends at home.

Finally, he turned toward her and reached for her

hand. His right hand rested in his lap, his arm still in the cast.

"I was happy with my life. I had my friends, my job, my church activities and my volunteer work. I stayed busy, and life was satisfying. Until you came. The more I got to know you, the more I began to see that something was missing. Something I had convinced myself that I didn't need. I was wrong."

He leaned toward her, tenderness in his eyes. If he was aware of the audience they now had, he apparently didn't care. "Remember when you asked me to show you what it's like to feel loved and cherished? I kissed you. And it shook me to the core. You know why? Because I meant it. Every bit of it."

Meagan released a breathy sigh. The audience was no longer forefront in *her* mind, either. Hunter had just in so many words told her he loved her. Her heart stuttered, and her stomach settled into a quivery lump.

He squeezed her hand. "I love you, Meagan. And if you're ready to give this thing a try, I am, too. Please come back to Cedar Key with me."

She opened her mouth, but the words stuck in her throat. Hunter had come for her. He was asking her to return with him. And he had just told her he loved her. In front of a dozen strangers. But there was one more thing she needed. Without it, she wouldn't go back.

"What about trust? You have mine. You've had it almost from the start. But if I don't have yours, it'll never work."

He drew in a deep breath. "I trust you, sweetheart. I see your integrity, your honesty and your selflessness. Lying goes against everything inside of you. I couldn't see that before. My pride got in the way. But now I know.

You're beautiful, inside and out." His gaze locked with hers and held. "Please come back with me."

Joy flooded her. Hunter had just given her everything she desired. "Yes, I'll come back."

Applause broke out, started by the clerk, reminding Meagan that they *did* in fact have an audience. Hunter stood and pulled her to her feet.

"Let's get that ticket cashed in."

When they reached the counter, the clerk already had the money counted out. "Good luck to you kids. I hope you find happiness." Her eyes locked with Meagan's as she tilted her head toward Hunter. "Honey, you need to get some help for that temper of yours."

"What?" She looked at Hunter. Then realization dawned, and she shook her head. "Oh, no, that wasn't me. He got shot. I didn't—"

Hunter began to laugh. With a hand on the small of her back, he guided her toward the door, still laughing. They stepped out into the October sunshine, and her own laughter mixed with his. Giddiness swept through her, an odd sense of weightlessness.

She had come to Cedar Key to escape. To live out her life alone, in safe obscurity.

Instead she had found love.

Hunter walked her to the truck, and she leaned against it, waiting for him to open the door. When he stepped closer and planted a hand next to her, her head swam. He didn't exactly have her pinned. His right arm was at his side, still in the cast. But even if he had had her totally caged in, she wouldn't have wanted to get away. His gaze was warm, everything he was feeling shimmering in those gorgeous blue eyes. This time she wasn't going to have to ask.

He leaned closer. The clerk was probably watching

through the window. Several other people likely were, too. But the moment his lips met hers, all other distractions faded into nothingness. There was only Hunter and his love and prospects for a bright and happy future.

Yes, she had walked away from everything.

And found so much more.

EPILOGUE

Nine months later

Notes from the pipe organ filled the large sanctuary, and Hunter shifted his weight onto his toes, then back again. Blake stood next to him, with Wade on Blake's other side, and finally Hunter's cousin, Phillip. The church was decked out with flowers, but nothing was overdone. The decor was simple but elegant. Just what he would expect from Meagan.

With most of Cedar Key on the guest list, along with his Ocala friends and family in attendance, they had chosen to hold the ceremony and reception in the large church in his hometown. It was a good thing. Every pew was packed.

The music changed, and Darci started up the aisle. She was wearing a light purple dress. No, not purple— Radiant Orchid, according to Meagan. She had corrected him several times. Radiant Orchid was *not* purple, just as salmon and mauve were not pink.

Meagan had put the whole wedding together herself. Hunter had always been impressed with her artistic ability. But watching her design and create floral arrangements, and set out in search of just the right piece of fabric or lace or other accessory for the image she had in her mind, gave him a new respect for her artistic eye.

When Darci was halfway up the aisle, another young lady followed—his sister, Amber. The smile she wore stretched across her face, and her eyes shone. When he'd announced his engagement to Meagan, Amber had been the most excited of anyone. At least she was the most vocal. She never ran out of energy. And rarely shut up.

The final bridesmaid coming down the aisle was Meagan's sister, Jennifer. Her dress was a shade of deep purple that also had a fancy name. He just couldn't remember it at the moment. A younger version of Meagan, she was struggling to hold back tears.

His gaze shifted to the right, where Meagan's mother sat. If she was fighting tears, she had apparently lost the battle, because hers were flowing freely, making twin trails down her cheeks. He understood. Both women were experiencing something they'd thought they would never see—Meagan on her wedding day, having been brought back to them from the dead.

Jennifer stepped onto the platform and grinned over at Amber. Since Meagan's mother and sister had moved to Ocala six months ago, Amber and Jennifer had become best buds.

Once all three bridesmaids were in position, mirroring the locations of the groomsmen, the music changed again, becoming louder, slow and deliberate. The mother of the bride stood, and the whole church followed suit.

Then Meagan appeared at the end of the aisle, her arm looped around Darci's father's, and the sight of her took Hunter's breath away. Soon he would vow to have and to hold her, to love her till death. And she would become Mrs. Elaina Kingston.

But to everyone in Cedar Key, and to him, she was

still Meagan. Though her bank accounts and identification said Elaina Thomas, Meagan had become somewhat of a nickname.

Everyone knew her story. And when Hunter encountered someone who didn't, he shared it. Because he was proud of her. Proud of her courage. Proud of the strength and determination that had kept her alive against all odds. Proud of the serene, confident woman she had become and the example she provided to the youth of the church in her position as an assistant to the director.

As she started down the aisle, her eyes met his through the sheer veil, and his heart almost stopped. She was beautiful. In the months since Edmund's capture, her hair had gone back to its natural blond color and had grown out to fall against her shoulders. But today it was up, woven with tiny flowers. And her green eyes were lit with a happiness that even the veil couldn't hide.

When Darci's father put Meagan's hand in his, Hunter's heart swelled with love and gratitude. In moments, he would recite his vows. But as he stood facing her, clasping both her hands, he made some silent ones of his own.

He would never take her for granted. Or saddle her with unrealistic expectations.

She was a precious gift, sent from God.

The only one able to heal his heart.

* * * * *

Dear Reader,

Thank you for joining me for a second trip back to Cedar Key. Every time I visit, I fall in love a little more with the place, and I hope you are, too. As was the case with *Shattered Haven*, most of the locations mentioned in this book are real places, although I did take a lot of artistic liberty with the Island Hotel Restaurant's bathroom.

After getting to know Hunter in the first book, it was fun writing his story. Meagan was enjoyable for me to write, too. She had a lot of strength and determination and did what she had to to stay alive. With her dark and deceptive past, she was the least likely woman to capture Hunter's heart, but once he recognized some faults in himself, he was able to open himself to love her in return.

I hope you'll come back to Cedar Key soon for Darci's story. In the meantime, I'd love it if you'd drop me a line. You can find me on Facebook (www.facebook.com/caroljpost.author), Twitter (@caroljpost), my website (www.caroljpost.com) and email (caroljpost@gmail.com). For news and exclusive content, join my newsletter. The link is on my website. I promise I won't sell your info or spam you!

God bless you!

Carol

REQUEST YOUR FREE BOOKS!
2 FREE RIVETING INSPIRATIONAL NOVELS
PLUS 2 FREE MYSTERY GIFTS

Love Inspired.
SUSPENSE
RIVETING INSPIRATIONAL ROMANCE

YES! Please send me 2 FREE Love Inspired® Suspense novels and my 2 FREE mystery gifts (gifts are worth about $10). After receiving them, if I don't wish to receive any more books, I can return the shipping statement marked "cancel." If I don't cancel, I will receive 4 brand-new novels every month and be billed just $4.99 per book in the U.S. or $5.49 per book in Canada. That's a savings of at least 17% off the cover price. It's quite a bargain! Shipping and handling is just 50¢ per book in the U.S. and 75¢ per book in Canada.* I understand that accepting the 2 free books and gifts places me under no obligation to buy anything. I can always return a shipment and cancel at any time. Even if I never buy another book, the two free books and gifts are mine to keep forever.

123/323 IDN GH5Z

Name	(PLEASE PRINT)

Address	Apt. #

City	State/Prov.	Zip/Postal Code

Signature (if under 18, a parent or guardian must sign)

Mail to the **Reader Service:**
IN U.S.A.: P.O. Box 1867, Buffalo, NY 14240-1867
IN CANADA: P.O. Box 609, Fort Erie, Ontario L2A 5X3

**Are you a current subscriber to Love Inspired® Suspense books
and want to receive the larger-print edition?
Call 1-800-873-8635 or visit www.ReaderService.com.**

* Terms and prices subject to change without notice. Prices do not include applicable taxes. Sales tax applicable in N.Y. Canadian residents will be charged applicable taxes. Offer not valid in Quebec. This offer is limited to one order per household. Not valid for current subscribers to Love Inspired Suspense books. All orders subject to credit approval. Credit or debit balances in a customer's account(s) may be offset by any other outstanding balance owed by or to the customer. Please allow 4 to 6 weeks for delivery. Offer available while quantities last.

Your Privacy—The Reader Service is committed to protecting your privacy. Our Privacy Policy is available online at www.ReaderService.com or upon request from the Reader Service.

We make a portion of our mailing list available to reputable third parties that offer products we believe may interest you. If you prefer that we not exchange your name with third parties, or if you wish to clarify or modify your communication preferences, please visit us at www.ReaderService.com/consumerschoice or write to us at Reader Service Preference Service, P.O. Box 9062, Buffalo, NY 14240-9062. Include your complete name and address.

LIS15

SPECIAL EXCERPT FROM

Love Inspired.
SUSPENSE

Can the Capitol K-9 Unit find Erin Eagleton and solve the mystery of her boyfriend's death before it's too late?

Read on for a sneak preview of
PROOF OF INNOCENCE,
the conclusion to the exciting saga
CAPITOL K-9 UNIT.

An urgent heartbeat pounded through Erin Eagleton's temples each time her feet hit the dry, packed earth. She stumbled, grabbed at a leafy sapling and checked behind her again. The tree's slender limbs hit at her face and neck when she let go, leaving red welts across her cheekbones, but she kept running. Soon it would be full dark, and she would have to find a safe place to hide.

Winded and damp with a cold sweat that shivered down her backbone, Erin tried to catch her breath. Did she dare stop and try to find another path?

The sound of approaching footsteps behind her caused Erin to take off to the right and head deeper into the woods. She had to keep running. But she was so tired. Would she ever be free?

Memories of Chase Zachary moved through her head, causing tears to prick at her eyes. Her first love. Her high school sweetheart who now worked as a K-9 officer with an elite Washington, DC, team. A team that was investigating her.

From what she'd read on the internet and in the local papers, Chase had been one of the first officers on the scene that horrible night.

She'd thought about calling him a hundred times over these past few months, but Erin wasn't sure she could trust even Chase. The last time they'd seen each other last winter, on the very evening this nightmare had taken place, he hadn't been very friendly. He probably hated her for breaking his heart when they were so young.

But then just about everybody else along the beltway hated her right now. Erin had been on the run for months. She knew running made her look guilty, but she'd had no other choice since she'd witnessed the murder of her boyfriend, Michael Jeffries, and she'd almost been killed herself. The authorities thought she was the killer and until she could prove otherwise, Erin had to stay hidden.

Don't miss
PROOF OF INNOCENCE
by Lenora Worth,
available August 2015 wherever
Love Inspired® Suspense books and ebooks are sold.

LISEXP0715

Love Inspired

Love the Love Inspired book you just read?

Your opinion matters.

Review this book on your favorite book site, review site, blog or your own social media properties and share your opinion with other readers!